Wyckford General Hospital

Small-town medics finding big love!

There must be something in the water in Wyckford, Massachusetts. The small and quirky town is brimming with dedicated medics and first responders who are at the top of their game.

The one thing they don't have is love. Some have had it and then lost it, some wanted to find themselves first and some have never felt they could have it... until now. They're all about to find themselves fighting to resist temptation... The temptation to have everything they've ever wanted!

Discover Brock and Cassie's story in
Single Dad's Unexpected Reunion

Read Tate and Madi's story in
An ER Nurse to Redeem Him

Follow Mark and Luna's story in
Her Forbidden Firefighter

Check out Sam and Riley's story in
Family of Three Under the Tree

All available now!

Dear Reader,

It's so hard to believe that this is the fourth and final book in my Wyckford General Hospital quartet. Seems like just yesterday I had the idea for my fictional little town on the shores of Buzzard's Bay and the brave first responders who live and fall in love there. But this is it! I'm wrapping things up with Riley Turner and Sam Perkins. These are two wounded people (both literally and figuratively) who are finding their way back to love and acceptance. We also meet Sam's adorable daughter, Ivy (bestie of Adi Turner, of course), and Sam's adopted mutt, Spork! Riley is coming to terms with her life postaccident and her future as a wheelchair user, and Sam is navigating life as a single father after the passing of his wife. I wish you all the magic of the season and hope you find as much joy and healing in life as Riley and Sam do in *Family of Three Under the Tree*. Until next time...

Happy reading!

Traci <3

FAMILY OF THREE
UNDER THE TREE

TRACI DOUGLASS

MEDICAL ROMANCE

Harlequin®
MEDICAL
ROMANCE

ISBN-13: 978-1-335-94271-5

Family of Three Under the Tree

Harlequin Enterprises ULC
22 Adelaide St. West, 41st Floor
Toronto, Ontario M5H 4E3, Canada
www.Harlequin.com

Printed in U.S.A.

Traci Douglass is a *USA TODAY* bestselling romance author with Harlequin, Entangled Publishing and Tule Publishing and has an MFA in Writing Popular Fiction from Seton Hill University. She writes sometimes funny, usually awkward, always emotional stories about strong, quirky, wounded characters overcoming past adversity to find their forever person and heartfelt, healing happily-ever-afters. Connect with her through her website: tracidouglassbooks.com.

To Charlotte,
the editorial steward of my first
seventeen books with Harlequin.
Thank you for all your guidance and support. <3

And to Annie,
my new editor guide:
Cheers to seventeen more together,
starting with this one! <3

CHAPTER ONE

DR. SAM PERKINS inhaled the pine-scented air as he walked up the curving sidewalk to his rental place in Wyckford, Massachusetts. For now, this house worked fine, even if it made his latent handyman skills itch to be used again. Renovating things relaxed him, and had helped him work his way through medical school while keeping him sane despite the crazy hours. Kept him going day to day as he worked on one project after another even as he slowly lost his beloved wife to ALS. Something about the smell of sawdust and fixing what was broken calmed and focused him the same way his patients and surgeries did. He'd always been a caretaker, first for his single mother as a kid, and now for his daughter, Ivy. It was what he did, who he was.

The approaching winter was still a novelty though. In San Diego, where he and his daughter had moved from two years ago after his wife passed away, the temperatures stayed consistently around seventy degrees and the skies were reliably clear and blue. Here, in Massachusetts in December, the temperatures fluctuated between cold and colder, and the threat of nor'easters could chill you to the bone. Last year, he'd been caught off guard by the snowfall. This year, even though Thanksgiving had just happened and there were no storms in the forecast, he was prepared with both a heavy-duty shovel and a snowblower, just in case.

He drew in another deep breath, hoping the crisp air would perk him up and dissolve the stress of the day. Since taking over as head of neurosurgery at Wyckford General Hospital this past September, his plate was beyond full, with what seemed like endless rounds office hours, emergency consults in the ER and follow-ups with the patients in his ALS research study. Amyotrophic lateral sclerosis was a progressive neurodegenerative disease that affected nerve cells in the brain and spinal cord. It had claimed his wife, despite Sam's valiant efforts to the contrary, and Sam was determined to find a cure, even if it was too late to save Natalia. He owed her that much for his failure.

Light snowflakes began falling, landing on his cheeks as he stepped up to his door. The neighborhood had a quaint, small-town vibe, with lots of well-kept homes, manicured lawns and even the occasional white picket fence. Very different from the modern, contemporary Mission Hills home they'd had on the West Coast, but still nice.

When Sam walked inside, the first thing that greeted him was the aroma of vinegar from kimchi and the earthy, miso-like scent of doenjang jjigae—a hearty Korean stew with vegetables and beef in broth. The second was their overeager mutt, Spork. He was part shih tzu, part schnauzer, and all energy. Sam toed off his boots and set them by Ivy's near the heating vent on the floor, then scratched the dog behind the ears. They'd adopted Spork from the local rescue shelter and the canine was settling in just fine, at least based on the number of toys scattered all over the house.

"Hi, Daddy," his daughter called from where she sat at the island in the kitchen down the hall. Ivy's backpack rested on the stool beside her and was almost as big as she was. Sam couldn't remember ever having that much homework in first grade, but apparently times had changed.

"Hi, *yeobo*," he called back, using his pet name for his daughter as he tossed his keys onto the side table then walked toward the delicious smells from his childhood, Spork still circling his ankles with his favorite octopus stuffed animal in his mouth. Sam gave Ivy a kiss on the cheek. "How was school?"

"Good. Adi and I got to pet an iguana today."

"Wow." Sam grinned as he turned to greet the nanny. "Hey, Hala."

"Mr. Perkins." The woman bowed slightly, her black hijab covering her gray hair. In her early seventies, she'd emigrated from Jordan to the US with her husband almost thirty years ago and had worked as a nanny ever since. She also did some housekeeping for Sam and picked Ivy up from school when he had to work late. They were lucky to have her, even if Hala had no qualms about giving Sam life advice whether he needed it or not. "Dinner should be ready shortly. I heated up something from the freezer."

"Thank you." Sam turned back to his daughter. "An iguana, huh? That sounds cool."

"It was!" Ivy swiveled slightly, her pink-stockinged feet tapping against the legs of her stool. "His name was Fred."

"Fred the iguana." Sam snorted. "Got it."

He moved the backpack to take a seat on the other stool. At least the kitchen in their rental had been updated. Quartz countertops gleamed under the recessed lighting, and new stainless steel appliances and freshly painted cabinets completed the modern decor. Sam wasn't the best cook ever, but he knew a few good recipes, most learned at the hip of his Korean mother, who'd insisted he learn to fend for himself when he went off to college. The others had been gleaned from Natalia's Italian heritage. An odd culinary mix but a tasty one. Meal prep, which Sam did on the weekends, was a lifesaver for him.

"Anything else interesting happen today?" he asked his daughter. His mom had always led with that question after school, and it felt like a tradition now. Sam's dad had left when he was just a baby, so it had always been the two of them. He'd gotten his first job as a bagger at a grocery store near their home after school when he'd been just thirteen to help pay the bills. "What did you learn?"

Ivy continued coloring the rainbow dinosaur in front of her. "I learned about butterflies and states and pastrami."

Sam glanced at Hala, who appeared to be holding back a laugh, before looking back at Ivy, confused. "Pastrami?"

"Yeah." Ivy nodded. "The stars are cool!"

"Oh. Right." Sam bit back a smile of his own. "You mean astronomy."

"That's what I said, Daddy. Pastrami."

Chuckling, Sam pushed to his feet and ruffled his little girl's hair. He was still wearing his scrubs from the hospital and needed to shower and change before dinner. "Be right back."

"Wait, Daddy," his daughter called before he'd made it out of the room. "I didn't tell you the most exciting part!"

Sam turned back, steeling himself for just about anything. "And what's that?"

"Ice, Ice Baby."

Sam frowned, leaning a shoulder against the

door frame, trying to puzzle out what that meant. "The song?"

"No. The town pop-up festival," Hala supplied helpfully. "The town has done it every year that my husband and I have lived in Wyckford. It's put on by the local town council once the weather gets cold enough to support an ice rink. The fire department sets it up in the town square. All proceeds go to support the local food bank."

"Can we go, Daddy? Please?" Ivy said, so excited she was practically bouncing on her stool. "I've never been ice-skating before and Adi's going and there's hot cocoa and Santa and please! I can't miss it!"

He sighed, still processing her stream-of-consciousness chatter. His first instinct was to say no. Standing around in the freezing cold after working at the hospital all day wasn't exactly Sam's idea of an enjoyable time. But Christmas was Ivy's favorite holiday, and they were trying to start a new life and new traditions here in town. And he couldn't let her down, especially when it was obvious from her excitement that she really wanted to go. Plus, he'd promised himself he'd make this year's holiday special for his daughter, so…

"Fine," he said, scrubbing a hand over his face. "When is it?"

"It's a secret," Ivy said, grinning.

"A secret?"

"They don't announce the dates ahead of time," Hala said. "It just pops up one day."

"Great." Sam wasn't a man who enjoyed surprises. In his experience, they were bad news.

"Yay!" Ivy ran over to hug his legs in appreciation before scrabbling back up on her stool to finish her dinosaur before dinner. "This is going to be the best Christmas ever!"

Sam really hoped that was true. They could use a bit of brightness and cheer after all the heartache in California, and he felt obligated to do his part to make that happen, even if he wasn't thrilled about it. He walked down the hall to the master bedroom and closed the door, then stripped before heading into his attached bathroom and stepping into the shower for a quick scrub and rinse. And sure, maybe he'd been told over the years that he could be a bit of a buzzkill because of his penchant for analysis and logic and detail, but those same qualities served him well when it came to his career—and to his skills as a caretaker. Seeing what people needed and fulfilling those needs. In truth, he honestly didn't care what other people thought. Living with a terminally ill person had taught him that. Losing Natalia had taught him the lesson that the important things in his life were his work and his family and protecting and serving those who relied on him. And perhaps he did use those duties as a barrier to keep people who weren't part of that circle away sometimes, especially after losing his wife. Better to avoid getting entangled with others than risk failing anyone else ever again. He had enough to handle with Ivy and his patients.

Letting people in, letting them help you, isn't a weakness, you know.

Those had been some of Natalia's final words to him before her passing. And while they were true, Sam hadn't been ready to listen then. Still wasn't ready to listen now. Relying on other people, allowing them into his life and heart, required a level of trust and vulnerability he never wanted to experience again. So, until further notice, he planned to stick to his status quo. Even if it was lonely sometimes.

He shut off the water and grabbed a towel to dry off, then padded into his bedroom to put on fresh jeans and a dark green sweater before pulling on socks and padding back to the kitchen to eat. Hala had just set dinner on the island and was serving them each up a bowl of stew and kimchi before getting one herself. Her husband wasn't picking her up until later due to a late shift at the hospital that night. He ran the hospital's environmental services department.

They chatted about their days while they ate, and Sam was grateful his daughter seemed to be settling in so well. She even had a best friend now. He took another bite of stew, ignoring the odd pinch of melancholy as memories of eating this same dish with his mother flooded in. He hadn't made many new connections in town himself, being so busy and all. But he was surrounded by people all the time at work, so it wasn't like he was a hermit. Plus, he chatted with his neighbors when he took Spork for walks. Or picked Ivy up from school. And while he often found himself awake at night and staring at the ceiling, wondering if the Natalia-sized hole inside him would ever heal, that was life, wasn't it? His mom used to tell him a bend in the road was not the end of the road. His life was different now than he'd expected, but he would make it work. He always did. Better than getting his heart stomped on and obliterated by grief. He was always the strong one, the dependable one, the person who took care of everyone else. The sooner he got over whatever this momentary bout of melancholy was the better.

Ivy needed him, and Sam didn't want any more complications in his life.

"Can I, Daddy?" Ivy asked, drawing him out of his thoughts.

Sam wiped his mouth with his napkin to hide the fact he hadn't been paying attention. "Can you what, *yeobo*?"

"Spend the night tonight at Adi's house after the meeting?" Ivy said. "Please? She said it was all right with her parents."

"I don't know." Sam frowned. It was a school

night, and sleepovers were usually restricted to weekends.

"Remember I have the day off tomorrow, Dr. Perkins," Hala added.

And Sam had a full schedule the next day, which would take him well into the night, so maybe it wasn't such a bad idea after all. "You're sure it's okay with her parents?"

"Yes, Daddy." Ivy gave him a solemn nod. "You can ask them yourself when you drop me off at the meeting."

"What meeting?" Sam had a feeling he'd missed way more of their conversation than he'd thought.

"The town hall meeting. Adi said you can bring me there, and I'll go home after with them."

"Adi said, huh?" Sam shook his head. His daughter's new best friend sounded about as bossy as her aunt. Dr. Riley Turner was a radiologist who often worked with Sam on the scans for his research study. While Sam got along fine with the woman on a professional level, that's where it ended. They exchanged pleasantries at work, discussed results after scans, and that was all. And the only thing he knew about these monthly town halls was that they were basically the small-town equivalent of reality TV, where everyone went to see and be seen.

Not exactly his cup of tea, but Ivy was still watching him, practically brimming with anticipation, so he finally gave in. "Fine. Now hurry up and eat so we can get you downtown."

People said you could never go home again, but in Riley's case, she'd never left.

At first, she'd stayed in Wyckford because she'd been too busy training to be a radiologist and rebelling against the rules her family had always imposed on her. Then later, following the car accident two years ago that had killed her parents and left Riley with a severe spinal cord injury, she'd been too sick. Even now, she was still trying to get back to the way her life had been before, working hard in PT with the hopes she might walk unassisted again someday.

For a long time, she'd imagined the most awful thing that could possibly happen to her would be living in her older brother Brock's shadow forever. But then the accident had shown her a whole new level of awful. Now she knew how precious life and freedom and independence were, and she didn't plan to give up any of them any time soon.

Riley rolled toward the entrance of the Wyckford Municipal Building for the monthly town hall meeting, carefully avoiding eye contact with all the people standing around outside for fear they'd want to help her. "The do-gooders," as she called them. She appreciated the sentiment, she really did, but she didn't need help. She did just fine on her own. Usually, Riley avoided gatherings like this so she wouldn't have to deal with them, but tonight she was meeting her Realtor here to discuss new places for Riley to look for potential residences.

Not that she didn't love and appreciate living at Brock's place, but the lack of privacy left a lot to be desired. Plus, with her brother now so stupidly happy in lurve, it left Riley feeling like a third wheel. Not that she wasn't thrilled for her brother and his new wife, Cassie, or her beloved young niece, Adi. But they'd recently had a baby too, so that made the house even more crowded.

And maybe it was her restless spirit, but Riley longed for space of her own, a new chance at life on her own. A chance to escape her brother's golden boy shadow once and for all after thirty-two years.

Not that she wasn't grateful for all Brock had done for her after the accident. He'd lost his first wife a few years prior and had been dealing with his grief and problems because of that, trying to raise Adi on his own while juggling their father's GP practice alone. Still, being together like that, grieving their respective losses, had brought them closer, healed old wounds and strengthened their sibling bond. But that phase was over and now Riley wanted something all her own, something unique and true and right. Something that would bolster her ability to take care of herself instead of relying on anyone else.

She paused at the threshold to take a deep breath before heading through the double doors into the chaos. The building was an old factory the town had renovated into a new useable space for their local government offices and meetings, thanks to a federal grant. The contractors had also made it fully accessible, so it featured wide halls, ramps everywhere there were stairs and an elevator up to the second floor, though that level was used mainly for storage these days. Riley smiled politely as she passed several townsfolk on her way to find an empty space to park her wheelchair. She'd come straight from her shift at the hospital, so still had on her green scrubs beneath her coat and comfy white sneakers instead of boots, and her long dark hair pulled back into a sensible ponytail.

As she traveled down the center aisle toward the front, she saw familiar faces in the rows lining either side, including Brock and Cassie and Adi. Cassie had mentioned earlier that they were leaving the baby home with a sitter. ER nurse Madi Scott and flight paramedic Tate Griffin were there too, as was Riley's physical therapist Luna Norton and her partner, firefighter Mark Bates. Mark was there in an official capacity as the newly appointed assistant fire chief, according to the agenda posted on the town's Facebook page, to discuss setting up the ice rink for the town's yearly pop-up holiday festival. She waved to each of them as she passed, praying she hadn't made a mistake coming here tonight. These things could last notoriously long as they turned into big spectacles, a chance for everyone to see and be seen, to voice their opinions— sometimes loudly—and catch up on all the local gossip, the town's biggest export—with Wyckford General as its main supplier. Given it was the largest employer in the area, most people either worked there or had family members who did, so it made sense.

Riley finally found a quiet spot near the far wall toward the front of the room and settled in for the show. At the very front of the space was a dais, on top of which was a long table where the town council sat. Lucille Munson spotted her from there and waved, her eye-wateringly bright pink track suit and lime-green headband on brand for the older woman. She was the queen of the busybodies in town and loved her shocking colors almost as much as she loved sticking her nose into other people's business. Riley plastered on a polite smile, the same one she used with difficult patients in the CT room, and waved a hand in response.

"Happy holidays, Doc," said a grinning security guard standing nearby. "Here, let me help you with your chair."

"No," Riley said, her tone sharper than she'd intended. "I got it, thanks."

The guard's grin faltered and he gave her a dubious look. "Might be easier if—"

"If what? If I let you handle things for me? Sorry, not gonna happen. I'm not here to make your life easier, Barry. And don't forget I punched you in the nose in kindergarten, and I'm not above doing it again."

His eyes widened slightly, and he looked like he was going to argue, but then Lucille called for him to help her with some supplies, so he had no choice but to rush off. Good. All Riley wanted at that point was a hot shower and a year-long nap. And yes, Christmas was coming up, but it was hard getting into the holiday spirit when you were exhausted all the time. Between her crazy schedule and frequent PT visits, Riley had virtually no time to herself these days. She searched the crowd for her Realtor, Lynette, but didn't see her. If she'd ditched Riley in this cheerful hell without telling her, she was going to… She pulled out her phone to check for texts. Yep, there was a message from Lynette. She'd gotten caught at a showing and couldn't make it. Said she'd call Riley tomorrow. Perfect. Grumbling, she shoved her phone back into her pocket.

She hadn't reached Scrooge territory yet this year, but she was close.

Ben Murphy, Cassie's dad, took a seat near Riley, greeting her and Luther Martin, the town curmudgeon who sat on the other side of him.

Now more than ever, Riley felt a kinship with Luther and his attitude. Sarcasm kept people at bay, especially the do-gooders. And while their situations were different—Luther was old while Riley was injured—people still tended to see them as less than, as needing assistance when they clearly didn't. It was infuriating. She appreciated their concern, but there were only so many pitying stares and platitudes a person could take. Her spinal cord had been damaged in the accident, not her brain, and Riley was still perfectly capable of taking care of herself.

She bent over to lock her chair wheels and when she straightened, Riley froze. What was Sam Perkins doing over by the entrance? Worse, why did her stomach flutter with invisible butterflies every time she saw him? She squashed them down fast, not wanting to feel that for anyone, let alone him.

"Everyone quiet down please," Lucille said into the mic on the table. She commanded the town council like a queen directing her lieges, and tonight was no different. "Thank you all for coming. On tonight's agenda, of course, is the pop-up Ice, Ice Baby festival, and we have Assistant Chief Bates with the fire department here to update us on their plans for this year's ice rink installation. We're also taking vendor sign-ups for the festival, so if you have or would like to make something to sell, please use the sheets at the back of room to get your name on the list. The exact date, as always, will be a surprise, but it'll be in December prior to the holidays, so you can plan accordingly. And finally, we'll discuss the suggestion of adding a new event to the festival schedule, the Ho-Ho-Horrorfest, and open the floor to public comments." A chorus of boos and cheers on the topic rang out before Lucille shushed them down. "Right. Let's get started."

Riley couldn't help watching Sam and his daughter as they hurried down the center aisle to take seats in the front row near Brock and Cassie. His little girl was as cute as a button, with the same dark hair as her dad but with green eyes instead of Sam's brown ones. She was best friends with Riley's niece, Adi. Other than the fact the man had arrived in town to assist Cassie with a patient's case and had never left, no one seemed to know much about him. Which was odd in a town where everyone knew everyone else's business. She'd managed to discover from Cassie that he was a widower and that he and his daughter had moved here from San Diego. Cassie had known and worked with Sam in California and had called him in to consult on the neurological aspects of a reconstructive surgery. Whenever Riley did scans for one of Sam's patients in Radiology, she and Sam always stuck to discussing the cases, never anything personal, which was fine. She'd had enough of people poking into her personal business a long time ago, even if she was curious about him.

Over the course of the next two hours, Mark walked to the head table and discussed the ice rink, then a myriad of townsfolk argued about the horror movie fest until Riley's eyes had glazed over. Occasionally, she glanced over at Sam to find him either whispering something to his daughter or staring blankly at the stage, probably fighting the same boredom-induced brain fog Riley was. He always seemed quiet and thoughtful and a bit tightly wound, which she found intriguing. And he was handsome, in a Daniel Henney sort of way. Before Riley's accident, he would've been just her type. But the last thing she was looking for now was romance. She didn't need anyone else in her life telling her what to do. Nope.

Then Sam looked over at her and their gazes locked, and for a brief second, a strange awareness passed through her, like warm honey on a summer's night—warm and sweet and comforting and...

Whoops.

The meeting ended and Riley hightailed it toward the nearest exit in record time, her heart racing for some stupid reason. Not fear exactly, but like she'd narrowly escaped a trap. A trap like Sam Perkins. She needed to get home and get some sleep—to get out of here before they did something stupid like start talking to each other socially. *Keep it professional, keep it safe, keep it free.* That was the way.

Bah humbug, indeed.

CHAPTER TWO

SAM WATCHED RILEY TURNER LEAVE, wishing he could do the same, but he still had to drop Ivy off with Brock and Cassie. He recognized lots of people here, both colleagues and patients, and he wasn't sure why she'd suddenly pinged on his radar tonight, but he didn't like it. He also shouldn't care that she'd kept glancing at him throughout the meeting, her gaze making the skin on his neck tingle with awareness. And then when he'd looked over and met her eyes and time had seemed to slow for some reason, it'd almost felt like…

Stop it.

He didn't want to socialize with Riley Turner outside the hospital. That could only lead to more talking and closeness and… No. He'd always appreciated people who were professional, poised and knowledgeable at their jobs. Riley was all those things to a T, and that was probably why she had a way of intriguing him that he hadn't expected and wasn't prepared for. It had nothing to do with her wheelchair. His wife had used one for the last year of her life, and Sam had become so used to it, he barely even registered them anymore. Plus, he saw how people at the hospital treated Riley, acting as though her disability superseded anything else about her. Natalia used to get so angry when people treated her that way. He knew Riley did too. He'd seen her tell several people off already for trying to push unwanted help on her.

A check of his watch said it was nearly 9:00 p.m. now, and people were slowly filing out of the meeting space. Sam took a deep breath, allowing some of the tension that had been building inside him since he'd locked eyes with Riley to dissipate. She was gone, and now he could get back to his comfort zone, his details. He had a penchant for being exacting to a fault with his cases, which frustrated some people, but if he was eventually going to find a cure for ALS, every single detail mattered. Every change in a patient's condition had to be documented and studied. And yes, maybe he insisted on being in control and having input into every decision in his research study. But he had to. It was his name on the reports, his professional reputation on the line. His patients depended on him. On some level, he knew he was using work as a barrier to keep the things that scared him—emotions, heartbreak, vulnerability—at bay, but he was okay with that exchange. What was a little loneliness if it meant peace?

"Daddy! Daddy!" Ivy tugged on his arm to get his attention. "We're ready to leave."

Brock Turner stood and stretched before smiling over at Sam. "I hope it's okay if Ivy stays with us tonight. Adi asked me late in the day, and I didn't have time to call you."

"Are you sure it's okay with you?" Sam asked.

"Fine." They knew each other from working together at the hospital. Brock was the town GP, as well as working in the ER when they needed extra help. He'd called Sam down for neurological consults on patients several times. And from what he'd gathered about the man, Sam knew Brock had been a single father himself—before being reunited with and marrying his old flame, Dr. Cassie Murphy—so they had that in common as well. Brock shrugged into his coat. "I'll make sure the girls get on the bus in the morning."

"And I'll make sure they have a good breakfast first," Cassie added, smiling as she helped Adi into her jacket. Ivy had never taken hers off. "I'm up early anyway with the baby, so…"

"Then I guess I'm good with it too. Thank you," Sam said, pulling his coat back on. "I've got a busy schedule tomorrow and my nanny has the day off."

"In that case, Ivy can come back to our place after school too, if you need," Cassie told Sam.

"I'm off, so I can spend time with them after school. You can pick Ivy up at our house after you finish at the hospital."

"Riley told me you worked with her on your research project." Brock chuckled. "Be careful. She can be salty when cornered."

Adi scrunched her nose. "What's 'salty'?"

Cassie ruffled Adi's hair. "Our cue to leave, that's what. Have a good night, Dr. Perkins."

Sam hugged his daughter. "Do you have all your stuff, *yeobo*? If you need anything, call."

Ivy grabbed the handle of her pink overnight bag. "I'm fine, Daddy. Stop worrying so much."

He touched his finger to the tip of her nose. "Worrying about you is my purpose in life. Please be good and don't make a nuisance of yourself. I'll see you tomorrow night."

"What's a *yeobo*?" Adi asked.

Sam laughed. "A Korean word that means 'sweetheart.'"

"Oh." Adi watched him curiously. "You're Korean?"

"Half," Sam said. "Ivy's a quarter."

Adi's eyes widened as she turned to her best friend. "You're money!"

"Come on, girls." Cassie herded them toward the exit. "For real this time."

"Right behind you." Brock gave his wife a quick kiss, and Sam felt a familiar pang in his chest. Despite his determination to remain alone, he still missed a lot of things about being married. It was the easy, casual shows of affection that most often got him in the feels: a lingering glance, a soft touch, a comforting word. All those little things that made a life complete.

"One more thing about my sister." Brock rocked back on his heels. "I know I said she was salty, and she is—especially when it comes to her injuries—but she's been through a lot the past couple of years and is struggling to find her way back to normal again."

Sam knew what that was like: having your future pulled out from under you and being left to search for any safe harbor. He was still processing his own loss himself, but he felt farther along than he had been. Moving across the country to come to Wyckford had helped. "Well, she's done excellent work with my patients, and that's all I care about. I'm sure things will be fine."

"Hmm." Brock seemed to consider that for a second before hurrying after his family. "Well, good luck to you. And whenever you need help with Ivy, just let us know. We're always happy to have her."

Sam couldn't imagine asking for help, especially with his daughter, but he filed the information away just in case. Then he headed home, alone this time. He missed Ivy's constant chatter almost immediately. He pulled into his driveway and saw the lights were still on, which meant that

Hala was still there, and felt immensely glad. He still hated coming home to an empty house.

"How was the town hall?" Hala asked when he walked in. She was knitting in the living room, waiting for her husband to pick her up. "Crazy as ever?"

"Since it was my first one, I don't have anything to compare it to." Sam plonked down on the couch, feeling exhausted. "But it was interesting."

"Interesting how?"

He told her about the meeting and mentioned seeing Riley there. He wasn't sure why.

Hala's knitting needles continued to fly with a speed and skill that could've given Sam's immense surgical skills a run for their money. "Dr. Turner's been through a lot recently. Everyone in town knew about her accident and helped support her and her family through the aftermath. You've been through a lot too."

Sam scowled. That was the second time someone had brought up Riley's past, and he didn't like it. He didn't want to be curious about her, didn't want to know more about her. "I'm sure she's fine. I am too."

"Are you?" A car horn sounded outside, and Hala finally looked up as she put her things into the tote bag near her feet, then walked to the foyer to pull on her coat and gloves. "I'll see you on Thursday. Good night, Dr. Perkins."

"Good night, Hala."

Alone at last, Sam locked up the house and shut off the lights, then went to bed. He stayed awake though, trying to get into the book he'd been reading, but his mind kept circling back to what Hala had said.

Dr. Turner's been through a lot recently. So have you.

Sam didn't want people's worry. He didn't want their interest either. He wasn't a sideshow exhibit. He just wanted to live his life as best he could now, moving forward and taking care of business and those around him just like he always did. Still, he couldn't shake the odd sense of connection he felt now that he'd realized that maybe he and Riley both had painful pasts they were recovering from. He wondered how she dealt with the pain, the memories, the isolation…

Frustrated with the direction his mind had taken, he shut off the light and went to sleep.

"Just a little longer, and we'll be done," Riley said through the speaker in the reading room to the MRI suite. She'd arrived early this morning to start the necessary scans before the patient's follow-up consultation. Daisy Randall was only forty-two, and she'd been diagnosed with ALS the previous December after nearly nine months of testing by various specialists. The patient's whole life and future had been shattered in the blink of an eye.

Riley could relate, which was probably why they'd become good friends.

Daisy's symptoms had started with a strange, sudden weakness in her left leg, which had progressed to a persistent limp. She'd seen GPs and physical therapists and several neurologists and had all kinds of scans and tests and treatments. Nothing had helped. Finally, she'd been referred to Sam Perkins for yet another opinion, and he'd given Daisy her definitive diagnosis of ALS. She'd enrolled in his research study shortly after that. Riley admired the woman's bravery and clear-eyed view of her future more than anything.

While a tech helped Daisy off the table in the other room and into the dressing area, Riley compiled the images from the completed MRI into the patient's digital chart for comparison with the previous set from her last follow-up visit six months prior.

"Sorry I'm late," Sam said as he walked into the dark reading room to view the images on the screen over Riley's shoulder. Suddenly being surrounded by Sam's scent of soap and spice, along with his warmth brushing her shoulder, had all the oxygen in the room disappearing for Riley. She tried to play off the ache in her chest as a cold. She didn't want to be aware of him. She vehemently did not want to get involved with anyone romantically right now, and Sam was a colleague, which made him strictly off-limits. It was bad enough she'd mooned over him at the town hall last night, where anyone and everyone could've seen. She wasn't sure what it was about him that turned her insides to goo, but she didn't like it. Not at all. Her life was complicated enough. She forced herself to concentrate on the work in front of her and not the muscular male body hovering near her right shoulder.

Get it together, girl.

Riley cleared her tight throat and began to relay the results to Sam in her best flat professional tone. "Objectively, Daisy's MRI results today are relatively stable compared to those from last time, with only slight hyperintensity increases in the CST and hypo-intensity in the motor cortex and brain atrophy consistent with the disease's progression. Subjectively, the patient reports worsening weakness in her legs, and she uses her wheelchair most of the time now for mobility. The tech will put her in the conference room at the end of the hall to go over the results with you."

"Right." Sam straightened. "What about you?"

"What about me?" Riley snapped before catching herself. He put her on edge. Another reason to steer clear. She took a deep breath and tried again. "Sorry. Long morning. Did you have more questions about the patient's scans?"

Sam crossed his arms. "No. I just know that you and Daisy are friends and thought she might appreciate having your support during the consult, since she's here alone today." He checked his watch. "If you're not busy, that is."

"Oh." Riley remembered the first weeks after the accident, all her subsequent surgeries and what a confusing time it had been for her. She'd relied heavily on her family to help her through it. Daisy's mother was moving to Wyckford from Boston to stay with Daisy, but it wouldn't be until after the first of the year. Riley swallowed the lump of guilt in her throat for the way she'd talked to Sam and checked her schedule on her computer. "Uh, actually, it looks like I am free."

"Great. I'll meet you in the consult room in five minutes." He started out then turned back. "Unless you need assistance—"

"I don't," she said, cutting him off.

Once he'd gone, she shifted in her chair, wincing slightly. The initial pain from her injuries as her nerves had slowly grown back together had gradually receded over the first few months until it was tolerable. On the worst days, she was entirely stuck in the chair. On the best days, she could walk at home with the use of a set of Lofstrand forearm crutches. But even now, after all her progress, if she sat too long, or stood too long, or forgot to stretch daily, or made any wrong moves—or basically lived, period—the pain could become debilitating. She used the chair at work and when going out in public because it was easier, though she hadn't given up on her dream of building up to the crutches full-time and doing away with the chair completely.

She rarely talked about what it was like for her these days, unless it was with someone who understood, like her physical therapist Luna, or Daisy. Otherwise, you ran the risk of people constantly telling you how strong and inspirational you were—or Riley's personal favorite, telling you that everything happened for a reason. Seriously? She wanted to scream at them, ask them what possible reason there could be for her parents dying and her being paralyzed. And the worst part of all was it was her fault they'd been out on the icy roads that night. The do-gooders meant well, she knew, meant to be comforting. But sometimes comfort came from just being there.

And she absolutely would be for Daisy now.

She went to lock her computer screen as her mind returned to Dr. Perkins. She hadn't expected him to invite her to the consult, but she'd be there for her friend no matter what. Also, she *really* hadn't expected him to treat her like the do-gooders tended to, and she didn't want him starting now. She had enough do-gooders in her life. It was weird because up until today, he'd never once treated her differently because of the chair. It was like he hadn't even seen it, which had been both odd and nice. Maybe that's why she'd suddenly developed her strange awareness of him the other night. Like a cat who always hung around people who ignored them.

Or pathetic losers who need to get a life. Or get laid. Or both.

Riley shook her head and pushed away from her desk. Dating was a whole other issue to navigate after her injuries. She'd been a bit of a hellion before the accident and had naively expected things to continue that way afterward. Then the first guy she'd been with after her spinal cord injury had freaked out during sex: getting her out of the chair, getting her back into it, all the stuff in between. A real mood killer. Since then, she'd taken matters into her own hands and used her trusty toys rather than risking humiliation and embarrassment with a partner again, even though sex was not just possible but enjoyable after spinal cord injuries, if done right.

I bet Sam would get it right.

Her traitorous brain put it out there before she could quash the idea. She had no business thinking about the guy like that, regardless of how he reacted to her chair.

Besides, Sam had never given any indication that he was even interested in her, or anyone else at the hospital for that matter, and it was none of her business anyway. She had enough to think about between her job and her recovery. Based on the latest reports from her specialists, Riley's long-term prognosis was still up in the air. Maybe she'd walk again on her own, maybe she wouldn't.

The funny thing was, despite it all, she still felt whole. Or mostly, anyway. But just because she was okay with her body as it was now didn't mean she could expect anyone else to be. And while her sex drive was as healthy as ever, what she missed most was the intimacy—lying next to someone, sated and sleepy, and falling asleep in their arms.

With a sigh, she started out of the reading room and down the hall for Daisy's consult. There, she found Daisy sitting alone on one side of a round wooden conference table while Sam fiddled with the large flat-screen monitor on the wall where the MRI imaging would be displayed. Riley smiled over at Daisy as she parked her chair at the table then reached down to lock her wheels, doing her best not to notice how Sam's green scrub shirt stretched taut over the rippling muscles of his upper back and shoulders, or how the sinew in his forearms flexed as he pressed buttons on the remote. Then Sam turned quickly and caught Riley's gaze, and something odd quivered in her belly.

Wow. Where had *that* come from?

She focused on the tablet she'd brought with her to see the scan notes on her screen, her cheeks hot as Sam took a seat a few chairs down from her.

"How are you feeling, Daisy?" he asked.

"Okay, I guess." The patient shrugged, looking defeated, and Riley reached across the table to take her friend's hand. "The past few months have been a lot, you know? I told my mom not to come today because I just need some time to myself. Since she moved back in with me, I don't feel like I have any privacy at all." She shook her head. "It's not her fault that I need so much more help with things now. And I know it's safer to not be alone. But I'm still processing, and I need space to do that. I thought things would get better with time as I adjusted and accepted my diagnosis, but all the stress and anxiety can still be overwhelming sometimes."

"That's perfectly normal," Sam reassured her. "Did you set up an appointment with the therapist I suggested? It can be helpful to talk things out with someone completely outside of the situation."

"I did," Daisy said. "The worst times are late at night, though, when I'm alone with my thoughts. Not knowing how much time I have left. You told me the average life expectancy is three to five years from diagnosis, but I've read about people who get less and some who get more. Stephen Hawking lived more than fifty years with the disease. And how long will I be able to talk and breathe on my own or eat without a feeding tube?" She dropped her head into her hand. "It's all so horrible and awful and incredibly unfair."

Riley squeezed Daisy's fingers. "You're right. It totally sucks. But please know I'm here for you, whatever you need, whenever you need. Call me in the middle of the night to talk, okay?"

Daisy looked up at her with a watery smile. "Okay."

Sam let a moment pass before clearing his throat. "Right. Are you ready to go over today's results and our plans for the next few months, Daisy?"

She nodded, and Sam started going over the MRI results while Riley found herself watching him again. He was good, explaining things in easy-to-understand ways, always with empathy and understanding for Daisy, even when talking in the most clinical terms. He seemed to trust his patients to ask questions as needed, and to know themselves and what they wanted for their care. They'd worked together on cases many times over the past year and a half, but for some reason he'd caught Riley's attention today and made her even more curious about him.

In a purely professional capacity, of course.

Then she looked over and found Daisy watching her watch Sam, and Riley immediately transferred her attention to the screen of her tablet again, but it was too late. Based on the look Daisy had given her, she'd thought Riley was ogling Sam, and now she'd have to explain that too.

Great.

At least Sam seemed oblivious to the situation, even as Riley stifled the urge to fan herself. When had it gotten so hot in the consult room?

"Pending the results of your PET scan next week," Sam continued, as he finished the slideshow of images on the wall monitor then set the remote control on the table, "I believe we can continue to monitor you for another six months with the same protocols in place. Any questions?"

"Not right now, Doc." Daisy squinted at her paperwork as Sam slid it across the table to her. "I'll have to drink more of that yucky contrast for the PET scan, won't I? It's in the separate building across the street?"

"Yes, and yes." Riley grimaced on her behalf. "But at least they keep the contrast cold, so the chalk taste isn't so bad. And I'll read the results with Sam when they come back before your next consult with Dr. Perkins. I can come to that follow-up meeting too if you want."

"Yes, please."

"Excellent." Sam stood and walked over to shut off the monitor, then patted Daisy on the shoulder as he passed behind her on his way to the door. "Let us know if you need anything. We're here for you."

"And I meant what I said about the middle of the night," Riley added. "Call me anytime it gets bad."

"Are you sure?" Daisy asked, sounding skeptical.

"Absolutely," Riley said, then rolled around the table to hug her friend as Sam left.

As she and Daisy embraced, their chairs clanking together, Daisy whispered in her ear, "I saw you eyeing my doc. He's hot, isn't he?"

"What?" Riley pulled back, flustered. "No. I mean yes. I mean, I don't know. I haven't noticed how Sam looks."

"Then you must be blind as well as paralyzed, girl," Daisy teased gently. "It's okay to like him as more than just a coworker. I know for a fact that he's single."

"Yes. His wife died," Riley said, sitting back in her chair. "And stop trying to set me up. I'm not interested in that right now."

Daisy gave her a flat look as they both headed for the door. "Whatever. I'd tap that if he wasn't my doctor."

Riley sighed as she turned off the lights in the conference room, then followed her friend out into the hall. "We are not talking about this."

Because the last thing Riley wanted to think about the rest of the day was tapping Sam or anyone else. But especially Sam, because she had a sinking feeling that she'd probably like it, and him, way too much. It was always the quiet, serious ones you had to look out for where your heart was concerned.

CHAPTER THREE

SAM SPENT THE rest of the day split between surgeries and more exams, including of several residents of the Sunny Village Retirement Home who'd come in with everything from neck and back pain to midstage dementia. He'd also performed an anterior cervical laminectomy and several lumbar punctures for testing.

The afternoon's highlight, though, had been an ER consult on a seventy-year-old patient brought in by her husband. She'd barely been conscious upon arrival, complaining of tingling in her extremities and mental fogginess. After all other medical conditions had been ruled out, Sam had been called. The ER had taken an extensive history and determined the patient was in good health for her age, and when asked about her activities that morning, she'd said she'd been cleaning the bar her son owned. Sam had just started examining the patient himself when the woman's son arrived carrying a paper plate covered with foil. Apparently, his mother had eaten several of the "special" treats while at his bar. The lab had confirmed the presence of THC in the woman's bloodstream, and they'd all had a good laugh over her just being stoned and not seriously ill. Sam had been relieved it hadn't been a stroke or worse.

After that, he'd headed back to his office to catch up on his dictation and spent the rest of the day there. Sitting back and yawning, he realized it was time to pick up his daughter at the Turners'.

The Turners.

Thoughts of the family brought back memories of that morning and how Riley had sat in on his consult with Daisy Randall. He'd known the two were friends, but seeing Riley be so supportive of Daisy had been touching. He would have given a lot to have someone like her around during Natalia's last days, when everything had been grim and hopeless. When they'd exhausted all possible avenues to keep her going. When death had been a blessing.

Get it together.

A familiar lump of grief and guilt constricted his throat as he pulled on his coat and packed it in for the night. It was silly to wish for things that would never be. It didn't matter whether Riley would comfort him in his time of need because that would never happen. He couldn't protect his wife. What made him think he could be trusted with anyone new in his life? Still, as he turned off the lights in his office and locked the door, he pictured Riley, with her long dark hair and bright blue eyes. The whole family, it seemed, had that same coloring, Brock and Adi included. Of course, on Brock it looked rugged, while on young Adi it looked innocent and sweet. And on Riley...

Sam sighed and rubbed his eyes. It didn't matter what it looked like on Riley. He tried never to think about his coworkers outside of work in anything more than a passing fashion. But for some reason, she kept creeping back into his head. Must be exhaustion.

Or perhaps it was her professional abilities. He'd always been impressed with people who were excellent at what they did, and Riley was certainly that. Earlier today, before Daisy's appointment, she'd noticed and pointed out things that he hadn't caught himself, a rare occurrence. She was smart and analytical and detail-oriented, a must for any medical professional. But his new fascination with her seemed to go beyond that, because the moments he remembered best about her had nothing to do with her brilliant radiology skills, and instead featured her kindness, compassion and heart shining through.

Sam grumbled to himself as he rode the elevator down to the first floor then walked out to his car in the parking lot. Natalia used to tease him about being a cold fish, claiming she'd melted the ice king's heart. But deep down, Sam felt things as strongly as everyone else. He just kept it hidden because that's what he'd learned to do growing up. His mother had needed him to be strong, to be the man of the house from an early age. He'd grown up young and shut off his emotions to provide for and protect those he loved. It was a sacrifice that had served him well. Those close to him knew he cared. He showed them in all the little things he did for them, in the way he held them and comforted them and did everything in his power to make their lives as easy and happy as possible. Then Natalia had died, and his sense of control had imploded. He'd had to become both provider and nurturer to his daughter while also processing his own grief. It was still a process, even now, but he tried to let his walls down with Ivy as best he could.

The problem he seemed to have now, though, was his emotions were bleeding through anyway these days, and usually at the most inopportune times. That was uncomfortable and unsettling. Sam didn't like to feel things too deeply. Emotions made one messy and vulnerable, two things he avoided being at all costs. And while his daughter needed his heart, she also needed his strength, and his patients needed his cool, calm, collected side. So, he compartmentalized as much as possible. Or at least he had, until these odd new reactions to Riley Turner had seeped in from nowhere.

For whatever reason, she had a way of getting under his skin now, in both good ways and bad.

Like at the town hall when they'd locked eyes. It'd felt like everything had disappeared except for her.

It was inconvenient, inexplicable and incredibly intoxicating.

Then this morning at Daisy's consult, she'd somehow worked her way even deeper into his psyche, with her healing smiles and her gentle hugs. There'd been a point when Sam himself had almost wished for her to hold his hand too, to tell him that he could call her anytime, just to talk or…

Enough. All this was ridiculous.

He stalked to his car. Even though it was only a bit after 6:00 p.m., the sun had set at least an hour before, another casualty of winter in Massachusetts. The days were so much shorter this time of year. Sam slid behind the wheel of his vehicle and started the engine, making another firm vow to forget about Riley Turner as anything more than a colleague, no matter how difficult a challenge that was proving to be.

By the time Riley drove home after work, used the power transfer seat in her specially equipped Chevy Traverse to get from the driver's seat back into her wheelchair, then down the ramp and out of the back of the vehicle, the whole process took a good ten minutes before she reached the front door. Adi and Ivy were there waiting for her, both wearing what looked like stretchy orange lamé balloons with fins and scales on them, and with holes cut out in front for their faces. She had no clue what those were, but it seemed like a Cassie problem, for which Riley was grateful.

As she passed the girls, she caught bits of their chatter, something about the yearly school Christmas play. In the kitchen, Winnie, the family's French bulldog, tried to bite her chair wheels again, but Riley got the dog's attention by tossing her favorite toy into the living room, then followed the canine in there to check her mail. All she wanted was a hot shower and a long nap. Unfortunately, what she got was her brother sitting on the couch watching TV. He didn't look away from his streaming show as she passed by.

"Long day?" Brock asked her, sounding polite but uninterested.

"Always." Riley sorted her letters into piles of bills and junk. "Did my Realtor call? She was supposed to be scouting new places for me to see, but she ditched me the other night at the town hall."

"Not that I know of." He finally glanced her way. "You know, there's no rush moving out. Take your time, find the right place for you."

"I appreciate that, but it's time." After all their losses the past few years, his generosity meant a lot to her. But she needed to get on with things, and while she understood her brother's protective nature, she didn't need a babysitter. Her life felt restricted enough as it was these days. "Where's Cassie?"

Brock sighed and turned his attention back to the screen. "Out."

"Hmm." Riley turned and headed toward the hall, where her bedroom was located on the right. Brock was a good man. But he was also annoyingly perfect, and everyone loved him. And how in the hell did you grow up next to *that*? Unfortunately, even as adults, Riley had sometimes still found herself playing the comparison game with Brock because all his successes had seemed like her failures. Then the accident had happened and given her a different perspective. In some ways, they were closer now than they'd ever been before. She still wanted a place of her own though.

Adi and Ivy followed Riley because the concept of boundaries didn't exist for seven-year-olds, and they stood off to the side while she changed into her pj's then went into her attached bathroom to take off her makeup. The builders had finished construction on Brock's new house shortly after Riley's accident, so he'd had them add all sorts of accessibility features for her knowing she'd be staying there awhile, including a wheelchair-accessible shower with a built-in seat that allowed her to transfer back and forth easily. The kitchen was also fully adapted to wheelchair height, with cabinets and counters that raised and lowered as needed. When she moved out, she'd either build a house on her own or do extensive renovations to retain all these special amenities, and they'd probably cost a fortune, but tonight she didn't have the bandwidth to think about it.

She'd just finished using her last makeup wipe when the doorbell sounded and both girls ran from Riley's bedroom, squealing with joy. From down the hall, she heard Ivy call, "Daddy!"

Which meant Sam was here.

Her pulse tripped without her consent. It made no sense, her reactions to him, because she had no reason to care if he was there or not. He'd come to pick up his daughter, no big deal. Still, she couldn't seem to stop herself from rolling out of the bedroom and down the hall toward the kitchen, her blood pounding through her veins. She rounded the corner just as Sam bent to pick his daughter up.

"Yeobo!" He kissed the little girl's cheek, his handsome face lighting up with joy, such a difference from his normal cool aloofness at work. "How was your day?"

"Good! Adi and I got picked to be goldfish in the holiday festival."

Ah. Goldfish, Riley thought. That's what those costumes were.

"And I told the teacher we'd babysit Fred over the holidays and—"

"Whoa, whoa." Sam frowned. "Who's Fred?"

"The iguana." Ivy gave him a look full of *duh*. "Remember? I told you about him the other day."

Riley bit back a laugh over the mental picture of even-keeled Sam wrangling an ornery lizard. Or at least she did until Brock turned and saw her in the doorway. Then her stomach sank. "Hey, sis. Can you come here a minute, please?"

She hadn't been expecting to see visitors and smoothed a hand down the front of her pink poodle-print flannel pj's and reluctantly went over to them, giving her brother a stern stare of warning. She wouldn't put it past him to do this on purpose to try and embarrass her. They might be adults, but old sibling tricks never went away, apparently. She glared at her brother, then said to Sam with as much dignity as she could muster, "Good evening, Dr. Perkins."

"Evening, Dr. Turner." Sam's tone held its usual crisp efficiency, though he was eyeing her pj's dubiously. "You look very…relaxed…tonight."

She bit back a snarky response, her face hot, then turned to her brother. "Did you need something?"

"Hey, girls," Brock said, looking completely unruffled in the face of her irritation, darn him. "Why don't you go get Ivy's things together?"

"Okay!" the girls said in unison, before racing off to Adi's room, leaving the adults in peace.

Brock waited until they were gone, then lowered his voice. "Sam asked where to buy presents locally for Ivy for Christmas."

She blinked at her brother like he'd grown a second head. They'd both grown up in this town. He knew as well as she did where to buy gifts for kids. She raised an annoyed brow at him. "And did you tell Sam where to go?"

"I did," Brock said, his hint of a smile setting off warning bells inside her head. Yep, this was a setup on her brother's part. She'd seen that smile before, when they were both in high school and Brock had gotten her a date with a guy who he'd thought would be "appropriate" for her, as in someone who wouldn't embarrass him in front of his friends. The date, with a math nerd who'd spent the evening explaining advanced calculus to her—and, yeah, it had been as exciting as it sounded—had been a total disaster. And now? Well, she had no clue what he was trying to do now, but she was sure she wouldn't like it. Especially if it involved Sam Perkins. The man might be hot, but his personality was as cold as Siberia as far as Riley was concerned. "And I thought it might be nice if you gave him a personal tour of downtown. Showed him where things are, that sort of thing. Be neighborly."

"I don't need a tour," Sam said at the same time Riley said, "Neighborly?"

If there was one thing that ground Riley's corn more than her brother being too perfect all the time, it was her brother trying to play matchmaker. He wasn't good at it. And who did Sam think he was, turning down a tour with her? She knew more about Wyckford than just about anyone. Indignant with both men, Riley glared up at them. "Brock, stop it. And, Sam, if you don't need help, why did you ask?"

"I didn't ask for help." Sam gave her brother a quick, reproachful look. "I asked for store names. I'm behind on my shopping and I like to support local businesses. Your brother came up with the rest himself."

Brock just shrugged before returning to the living room, infuriating Riley even more. What... the...?

Tempted as she was to tell them both where to park their sleighs and how to get there, she decided that poor Ivy shouldn't have to suffer with bad gifts because the men in her life were idiots. So, she took a deep breath and tried to sound as calm as possible. "I'll text you a list of stores if you give me your number."

Sam stared at her. "You want my number?"

Seriously? "Look, I get that you might think you're the town's hottest bachelor or something, but I am not interested, okay? You asked for names, I'm going to give them to you. That's all."

Tiny dots of crimson stained Sam's high cheekbones as he fumbled to pull his phone from his pocket. Good. That would teach him to make assumptions about people. And to think she'd thought he was different. As if she'd want to date him! She didn't want to date anybody. She didn't need a man to make her life complete. She didn't need anyone. She...

He cleared his throat as he frowned down at his screen. "I'll need your number first so I can text you mine. And to be clear, I don't want to date you either. I have more than enough going on in my life without romance."

"Same," Riley agreed, crossing her arms as she rattled off her digits for Sam.

Afterward, they both lingered there awkwardly, looking anywhere but at each other until Sam finally cleared his throat and hazarded another glance at her. "Nice pj's, by the way."

"Thanks." Riley raised her chin and gripped the arms of her chair, feeling oddly flustered and achy now, though she wasn't sure why. It certainly had nothing to do with the man in front of her. "They were a gift."

For a moment, their gazes held, and time grew taut, just as it had the other night at the town hall.

Weird how that kept happening when he was around.

Before Riley could contemplate it too long, though, Ivy called from down the hall, breaking the spell. "Almost ready, Daddy."

Sam snapped out of it, looking as perplexed by the situation as Riley felt. He studied the toes of his boots like they were the most interesting thing in the world. "I'll keep an eye out for that list then.'

"I'll send it as soon as I get back to my phone." She took a deep breath then turned back toward the hallway, calling over her shoulder, "Have a good night, Dr. Perkins."

Sam looked up at her again, this time with a small smile playing at the corners of his lips— one that sent her stupid pulse stumbling again. "Good night, Dr. Turner of the pink poodle pj's."

Riley blinked at him. Was that a joke? Was stoic Sam Perkins trying to be funny? Unsure how to handle that, she continued down the hall toward her bedroom as the girls raced past her on their way to the kitchen, orange fish suits glinting under the overhead lights.

Dr. Turner of the pink poodle pj's...

She couldn't help smiling as she rolled into her bedroom and shut the door behind her. Maybe there was a regular guy under his pristine professional facade after all.

CHAPTER FOUR

RILEY PUSHED HER wheelchair toward the only table left available in the corner of the Wyckford General Hospital cafeteria, her eyes fixed on the steaming tray of mac and cheese balanced on her lap. The last thing she wanted was hot food all down her front. Normally, she went for something healthier, but the rich entrée was the only meal option left at three in the morning, unless you wanted a wilted salad. Of course, the fact it was also her favorite comfort food didn't hurt either. It had been a busy, stressful couple of hours on the night shift, with several emergency cases from the ER due to a car accident, so she needed the break. Her stomach growled in anticipation as she reached her spot amidst a sea of others that were already closed off for the cleaning crew and maneuvered her chair into place.

She glanced around the space, the hum of vacuums and the smell of floor polish from the cleaning crew working in the area comforting, grateful for a bit of solitude. As a radiologist, Riley didn't have a problem being alone. She spent most of her days in a dark room staring at X-rays and scan images on her computer screen. And the night shift was usually quiet and allowed her time to surf the net between patients or read during her downtime. It also allowed her to mostly avoid the dreaded do-gooders, like the lady from behind the register who was making a beeline for Riley now.

"Here, hon," the woman said, the name badge pinned to the front of her white cafeteria uniform proclaiming her name was Madge. She was obviously new because all the others knew better than to approach Riley without her expressly asking for assistance. "Let me help you with that."

"I'm fine," Riley said, flashing the woman a tight smile. "I got it."

The woman scoffed and took the tray from Riley anyway, laying out her plate and silverware like she was four instead of thirty-two. Riley ground her teeth through it all, determined not to snap at the woman, but drew the line when the woman picked up the napkin and started toward Riley's collar like she needed a bib.

"Touch me and die," she growled low, causing the woman to halt midway, the napkin dangling from Madge's fingers like an SOS flag as her startled eyes widened. "I said I'm fine."

Madge slowly straightened, her surprised expression giving way to affront. "Well, I never. I was only trying to make life easier for you."

"You know what would make life easier for me?" Riley asked. "If people like you treated me like a grown, capable adult instead of a child. Now, if you'll excuse me, my dinner is getting cold."

She faced the table as Madge walked away, the woman muttering under her breath about ungrateful people and how rude Riley had been.

Maybe she was right. Maybe Riley had been rude. But then no one was trying to infantilize Madge because she was differently abled than other people. One of the few things Riley still had left from her old life was her independence, and she intended to keep it.

She'd just picked up her fork and was about to dig into her food when the sound of footsteps approached from behind her once more. If that was Madge returning for round two in the Do-Gooder Olympics, Riley might just have to scream. Then the footsteps halted next to her table and a familiar masculine voice asked, "Mind if I join you? I promise to treat you like a big girl."

Oh, man.

Skin prickling with heat, Riley slowly looked up to see Sam standing there with a tray of food in his hands. She'd forgotten he was working the night shift too. They'd seen each other earlier in the ER when she'd run down some stat films for one of Brock's patients. They'd given each other a polite nod in passing and she'd thought that was the end of it. But no, here he was, invading her personal space again. Like he hadn't been doing that anyway since the other night in the kitchen. She'd found herself thinking about him at the most inopportune times, like in the shower or when she was trying to fall asleep, and it was beyond annoying. She didn't want to think about him like that. She didn't want to wonder what he was doing or where he was. And she certainly didn't want to be attracted to the guy, even if he was tall and handsome, with a guarded look in his eyes that made her inquisitive side yearn to know more. But she'd also reached her brusque quotient with Madge, so she had nothing left. She shrugged and kept eating. "Go ahead."

Sam raised a dark brown brow then slid into the seat across from her. "Thank you. And thanks for the list of stores you sent me."

Riley gave a curt nod, feeling a bit grinch-y now. Sam was back in professional mode tonight, thoughtful and logical and exceedingly polite. And while it might work well with his patients, for some reason it was driving her batty now. Maybe because it made her want to ruffle him up. She'd always preferred life a bit more on the spontaneous side. Or at least she had until her wild side nearly cost her everything. She concentrated on what he'd said rather than the way his feet brushed hers under the table. "Hope it helps."

He continued fixing his wilted salad, carefully tossing the dressing with the veggies so none spilled over the side of the plate. "I'm sure it will, once I find out where they're located."

Riley snorted. "Wyckford isn't that big. You can walk through the entire downtown in twenty minutes on a bad traffic day. You'll find them."

Sam harrumphed then dug into his own dinner.

Silence stretched between them, only interrupted by occasional chatter from housekeeping around them. Riley snuck glances at him as she ate, until finally Sam said, "So, about the hit-and-run case from earlier tonight... I just got off the phone with the officers who responded to the scene. It seems they found a piece of fabric caught on a nearby fence that they tracked down to a Tucker Larson. They also found debris from his truck at the scene."

"Doesn't surprise me," Riley said. "The Larson boys have been trouble around Wyckford for years. Tucker, the older and healthier one of the two, is usually the ringleader. Lance, the younger one, has cystic fibrosis. He's smaller and frailer, but still a troublemaker. They caused some trouble out in the forest a few months ago. Mark Bates and the police caught them." She shook her head, stabbing her fork into her mac and cheese. "Up until now, they only posed a danger to themselves. It seems that changed tonight." Thoughts of the woman in the ER who'd been struck by their vehicle then left behind like roadkill infuriated Riley. She hoped this time the police locked them both up for a good long while. "Why do people think they can get away with stuff like that?"

"No clue," Sam said, wiping his mouth with a napkin. "Thankfully, the victim should make a full recovery. And the officers are already searching for the Larson brothers. Good thing too since they sound dangerous."

"They are," Riley said. "And that accident happened near the school too. Imagine if it had been a child instead."

Sam visibly shuddered. "Don't want to. If anything happened to Ivy, I'm not sure what I'd do."

His demeanor shifted then, true emotion breaking through, and it was such a transformation that Riley had to tear her gaze away from him to avoid gawking. His dark eyes took on a mesmerizing heat, and his voice grew husky and deep. She couldn't help imagining other times when he might lose control like that, and whew…when had it gotten so hot in there? She avoided fanning herself by shoveling more food into her mouth.

"What do you know about reptiles?" he asked her out of nowhere.

Stunned out of her unwanted lust, Riley swallowed. "Excuse me?"

"Reptiles," Sam said before taking another bite of his salad. "My daughter has apparently volunteered us to watch the class pet over the holidays, and based on my call to the teacher to try and get out of it, it's apparently too late to change it. So, I need to figure out what to do with an iguana."

"Oh. Right." She'd forgotten about that little snippet from the other night and this time she couldn't hide her grin. "Don't worry. Fred isn't much trouble. We kept him last year and all he did was eat and poop. And sun himself on the branch in his cage for a week."

Sam looked intrigued now. "What did you feed him?"

She used her fork to point toward his salad. "They're herbivores, so greens and some fruit. We gave him collard greens and kale. And a bit of banana and grapes, though that's more of a treat than regular food. You can google it too."

"That was going to be my next step, after talking to someone who knew what they were doing." He gave her a half smile and her heart squeezed a bit. "Ivy's so excited about it."

"She's adorable," Riley said, smiling herself. "I'm glad the girls found each other."

"Me too," he said, finishing up his salad. "Friends are important."

"They are," she agreed. She wasn't sure what she'd do without her friends here in Wyckford,

Luna and Cassie and Madi and Daisy. Probably go insane.

"With Fred off my list, now I just have to worry about the gifts for Ivy."

"You're a list kind of guy, aren't you?" Riley said before she thought about it. Whoops. Talking to Sam was easier now than she'd expected since he'd loosened up a bit. Maybe too easy. "Sorry. It's none of my business."

He chuckled and she felt the sound straight to her toes before she could stop it. "No, you're right. I am a list guy. It's what keeps my life running smoothly. Otherwise, total chaos."

"I get it," she agreed as she pushed her empty plate aside. "Though a little chaos can be fun sometimes too."

The minute the words were out, she wanted to take them back. That had come out way more flirty than she'd intended if the look Sam was giving her now was any indication, his dark eyes inscrutable.

Yeah. Time to go.

Riley wheeled away from the table to put her dishes on the conveyor belt nearby, leaving Sam to stare after her while she wished the floor would open and swallow her whole.

She'd hoped for a quick escape, but unfortunately the odds were not in her favor.

"Chaos, huh?" Sam said, placing his things on the conveyor belt after her then following her out into the quiet hall. "That's more your style? Never would've gotten that from your work. You're more anal than me when it comes to documentation."

"Have to be," she said, pushing the up button for the elevator, glad this was where they would part. She'd go back to the third floor, he'd walk to the ER on the other side of the building and her humiliating foray into flirting with the last man she should have would be over. "Keeps the malpractice vultures away."

What the hell was I thinking?

"True." Sam seemed to hesitate before saying, "Thank you."

Riley frowned, even more discombobulated now. The guy had somehow managed to knock her completely off balance without her even noticing. "For what?"

"For letting me eat with you tonight," he said, flashing a smile that would've melted her insides to goo if she'd been that type of woman. Which she absolutely wasn't, but still. "And for the advice on Fred. And for the list, again."

"You're welcome," she said as the elevator finally dinged, thankfully. "I'll see you around."

"Of course," Sam said, and turned away as Riley rolled onto the elevator.

She'd just pressed the button for the third floor and the doors were closing when a hand shoved between them, stopping them. She fumbled for the correct button to open them again and was shocked to see Sam there. He looked flushed and uncomfortable and as awkward as she felt, and her heart went out to him a little bit more.

"Uh, sorry. I just… Well, I don't have much free time, as you know. And with my schedule it would be hard for me to lose more than a day to shopping and I've been considering the offer your brother made the other night and…"

The elevator beeped angrily as he blocked the doors, cutting him off.

Riley shook her head. "What are you trying to ask me, Dr. Perkins?"

"I wondered if you might still consider showing me around downtown?" he said.

Shocked, Riley wasn't sure how to answer at first. The last thing she needed was more private time with Sam, considering how he seemed to do a number on her senses without even trying. She really needed to do something about that. But she also felt kind of sorry for him too.

Friends are important.

She couldn't help thinking that maybe he didn't have many around here, being new to town and all. Looked at that way, showing him around might just be her civic duty. That's the excuse she settled on anyway, against her better judgment. Maybe her impulsive side wasn't dead after all. "Okay."

"Okay?" he repeated, sounding as surprised as she felt by her answer. He coughed then and pulled out his phone, still blocking the whining elevator doors. "Okay. What's your schedule like this weekend?"

"I have Saturday off, but I'm working Sunday."

He nodded, typing on his phone. "Saturday then? I'll have to see if Hala can watch Ivy for a few hours. And I can drive."

"No. I'll drive," Riley said. "Text me your address. And bring Ivy along. I'm sure Adi will be thrilled to have more time with her bestie. And it'll give you an idea of the kinds of things to get for gifts too."

"Right." Sam nodded. "Okay. Saturday it is then."

"Yep." Riley still felt a bit stupefied by it all but smiled anyway. "See you then."

"See you." Sam finally stepped back and the elevator doors shut, leaving Riley alone with her spinning thoughts. What had she just gotten herself into?

Sam walked back to the ER to check on his consults in a bit of a daze. Why had he done that?

The only excuse he had was momentary insanity. What other explanation could there be for him charging back to that elevator to ask her to give him a tour of a town the size of a postage stamp that he was more than capable of exploring himself in just a few hours?

He shook his head as he walked through the automatic sliding doors and back into the controlled chaos of the ER. Didn't matter the size or location of a hospital, there always seemed to be people in need of medical attention, and Wyckford's was no exception. Residents and nurses bustled around, wheeling patients here and there, the smell of disinfectant sharp in the air. Considering his actions with Riley just now, perhaps he should have himself checked out. But beneath his confusion and self-recriminations, a low-level electricity buzzed through his system, an anticipation he hadn't felt in a long time—thought he might not ever feel again. And that was even more unsettling to him than making a fool of himself in front of Riley.

"Hey, Dr. Perkins," Madi Scott said from behind the nurses' station as he passed. "Got those labs back on the hit-and-run victim."

"Thank you," Sam said, stopping to look, grateful for the distraction. Her levels were improving, which was good. They would keep her overnight for observation, but with luck she could go home tomorrow. "See if you can find a room for her upstairs. I want a twenty-four-hour admit."

"Will do, Doc," Madi said, flashing him a bright smile. She was one of those perpetually perky people that he always marveled at. Natalia had been that way too. Sam didn't get it, but he appreciated it. "Everything okay with you?"

"Fine," he said, eager to get out of her spotlight. "Just tired."

Not a lie. He was currently working on four hours of sleep. He'd stayed up late the night before helping to finish Ivy's science project for school. He'd made enough construction paper germs to last him a lifetime. Now all he really wanted was to find an empty on-call room and curl up on the tiny twin bed there for an hour or two.

Unfortunately, it wasn't to be. A brawl at the local bar, Wicked Wayz, had led to two new arrivals, one with a serious concussion from whacking his head against a pool table following a fall after being punched. Of course, his blood alcohol level complicated matters as well. They had to keep him for observation just to let him dry out before they could reevaluate his condition.

Sam eventually made his way to the small staff break room in the department for a dose of caffeine and quiet, only to find Brock Turner in there as well, scarfing down a bag of chips and an energy drink from the vending machines. They were the only two in the room.

"Hey," Brock said when Sam walked in.

"Hey." He made a beeline for the coffee machine, shoving a pod into the thing before filling it with water and hitting Start. "Busy night."

"Always." Brock tipped his head back, dumping what was left of the chips into his mouth before tossing the empty bag into the trash nearby.

"Listen, I'm sorry about what happened the other night at my house."

"What happened?" Sam asked, shooting him a confused scowl over his shoulder.

"You know, about the whole tour thing," Brock clarified, looking a tad guilty. "I wasn't trying to set you two up or anything, I swear. I just thought it would be a good idea is all. Sorry if I made you uncomfortable."

Given that Sam had just finalized that very tour with his sister, he wasn't sure how to answer. He nodded and shrugged. "It's fine."

Next thing Sam knew, Brock walked over and slapped him on the shoulder. "If you ever want to talk, about work or whatever, I'm around. I know what it's like. Raising a kid on your own after losing the person you thought you'd share forever with."

Sam sighed and looked down at his hands. He had always been a private person, and he didn't want to burden anyone with his personal problems. But man, he was tired. And when he got tired, his barriers weakened. That's probably what had happened with Riley in that elevator. He'd been fighting his attraction to her for a while and tonight it just got out of hand. It had just been so nice to have company, someone to talk to who didn't pity him or worry about him or expect anything from him other than conversation. He hadn't realized how much he'd missed that until tonight. It could have been anyone across that table. But then he remembered her gorgeous blue eyes and inquisitive face and knew that wasn't true. He didn't want to talk to just anyone. He wanted to talk to Riley. She was snarky, yes, but she was also a blank slate, with none of his past guilt or sorrow thrown in to muddy things. Being with her felt fresh and new and clean. It made him feel hopeful, and wasn't that something? Another emotion Sam thought he'd never feel again after losing Natalia.

The coffee machine beeped, and he took his cup and turned to find Brock still standing there, waiting for an answer. Treading carefully, he said, "Uh, thanks. I appreciate it. And don't worry about the tour. Riley and I just made plans for Saturday to tour downtown, so no harm done."

"Really?" Brock looked impressed. "Wow."

Sam had figured it would come out sooner or later anyway in this town, so best to be up-front. They weren't doing anything wrong. It was just a tour. He sipped more coffee to dislodge the silly lump of excitement lodged in his throat. It *was* just a tour. Nothing more.

"Oh, nothing," Brock said. "I'm just surprised you got her to agree is all. She's been a bit withdrawn since the accident."

Sam had heard brief accounts of what had happened the night Riley had been injured through the hospital grapevine, but he wasn't one to put much stock in gossip and it felt like an invasion of privacy to learn the details from anyone other than her, so he didn't ask Brock more about that. If Riley wanted him to know, she'd tell him herself. "Well, in my professional experience with her, she seems fine. And it's just a quick tour of downtown. Shouldn't take more than a few hours. And Ivy's coming too. Riley said she'd ask Adi if she wanted to come."

Brock chuckled. "Good luck then, my friend." He clapped Sam on the shoulder again as he continued out of the break room. "I need to get back to work. And have fun Saturday."

Taking a seat at one of the small round tables, Sam pondered what Brock had said. The times he'd been around Riley during cases, she'd seemed anything but withdrawn—a bit abrasive with him, maybe, but Sam had never minded that. In fact, he liked people with a fighting spirit. He admired Riley's intelligence and gumption. He thought of her sitting across from him in the cafeteria, her long dark hair pulled back to reveal her neck and a small golden heart dangling from a chain dipping into the V-neck of her scrub top. Whenever she'd leaned forward to take a bite of food, that top had gaped open a little more, revealing a hint of the curves beneath, that little gold heart gleaming like a beacon. He wondered what it would be like to hold her, feel those curves pressed against him, kiss her lips, hear her sigh his name as he pleasured her...

Stop it.

Yeah, he was losing it big-time tonight, first running back to ask her to take him on a tour and now fantasizing about her in the break room. He needed sleep and a shower and perhaps a lobotomy. Not necessarily in that order.

"Dr. Perkins?" Madi called from the doorway. "Found the patient a room. Just need you to sign off on it."

"Great, thanks," Sam said. He downed the rest of his coffee then stood, doing a full-body shake like Spork did every night after his walk, trying to get his mind refocused on work and not Riley Turner.

One brought him calm and clarity, the other chaos and confusion—and no small amount of desire, misplaced as it was.

Madi left and Sam started to follow her out, wondering if it was too late to back out of Saturday, but no. He'd look even more foolish changing his mind again. She was already probably wondering what was going on with him. Better to keep the date-that-wasn't-a-date and do the tour then be done with it—and her—once and for all.

As he'd told Brock, it was only a few hours. He could control his inappropriate lust where she was concerned for that long. Of course he could. Knowing the girls would be there as well helped.

He wouldn't do anything crazy in front of Ivy or Adi, like try to hold Riley's hand or put his arm around her or kiss her. Nope. All of that was off the table. He was an adult. A parental figure. A role model for his daughter, not a hormonal teenager.

He'd lost Natalia, the woman he'd thought he'd spend the rest of his life with, the woman he'd failed to save, despite his years of medical training. He'd never been able to do enough to help his mother growing up either. They were always just squeaking by, money-wise. With school and a part-time job and trying to keep his grades up to get a scholarship for college, he hadn't been able to help her around the house like he should have. He hadn't been enough for them, plain and simple.

No reason to think he'd be enough for Riley now either.

Looking at it that way put a quick kibosh on his libido.

Now if he could just remember that on Saturday, he'd be all set.

CHAPTER FIVE

SAM AND IVY were standing on their front porch when Riley arrived to pick them up bright and early on Saturday morning. It had snowed a little the night before, so everything had a fresh coat of white. They climbed into Riley's specially appointed SUV, Sam in the front passenger seat, and Ivy in the back with Adi.

"Daddy, we're going to have so much fun!" Ivy squealed from the back seat.

"Sure," Sam said, with as much excitement as a kid finding coal in their stocking. Despite giving himself another pep talk this morning while he'd gotten ready, seeing Riley pull up had given him serious reservations about spending a few hours with her outside of work. Images of her in those silly flannel pj's kept popping into his head at the most inopportune moments, which then led to thoughts of her taking said pj's off to reveal her naked body, which had kept Sam up most of the night, tossing and turning, hot and bothered and completely baffled.

None of this was Riley's fault. She'd obviously not been expecting to see anyone that night at her brother's house and had just been going about her business. No. If anyone was to blame, it was Sam, for going along with her brother's scheme. He still couldn't quite fathom why he hadn't put a firm end to things, except for that moment—only a few seconds, really—where he'd looked into Riley's eyes and felt…pain and passion and a profound sense of fate.

Yeah, he had a problem.

If he hadn't been sitting in a car with other people, he would've smacked himself.

Sam did not believe in fate. Sam believed in logic and facts and hard work.

So, he concentrated on buckling his seat belt to distract himself from what could be early-onset dementia or possibly a stroke inside his head. Something had to be happening in there for him to be going off the rails like this and waxing poetic about a woman he'd sworn he wouldn't pursue. He couldn't trust himself not to fail someone again like he had Natalia and his mother. He had a hard enough time keeping up with Ivy these days. He needed to stick with his work and his quiet little family life at home. That was all. No muss, no fuss. No chance of losing anyone again.

Right?

Right. Which meant he needed to stay on the straight and narrow where Riley Turner was concerned. Yes, they'd had a nice conversation in the cafeteria the other night, and yes, maybe she'd flirted with him a little bit—he still wasn't sure about that. But that was no reason to go off the deep end each time he saw her. He couldn't walk around in a constant state of...*whatever* this was...for her. They'd have a nice couple of hours around town, then go their separate ways. It was for the best all around.

Therefore, as they headed downtown, Sam focused on the passing scenery, not his inappropriate awareness of Riley behind the wheel beside him, all pink-cheeked and fresh, sparkling like a shiny new ornament. People had swapped out their turkeys and pumpkins post-Thanksgiving for lights and trees and inflatable snowmen and other assorted creatures, to the point that it looked like the entire town was decorated to within an inch of its life. The new added layer of snow gave the whole town an old-fashioned, Hallmark movie kind of feel.

Eventually, they parked near a large plaza outside the local attorney's office. Barricades were set up around a large flatbed truck with what had to be the world's largest evergreen strapped to the back.

"This is where the town tree lighting takes place during the pop-up festival," Riley said as she maneuvered from the driver's seat back into her wheelchair. "They drain the fountain and set up supports inside it to hold the tree securely."

She then rolled down the ramp that bisected the seats in the vehicle and out the back doors of the SUV, which had automatically opened with the push of a button on Riley's key fob. Sam's wife had had a similar setup in her car back in California.

He got out too, helping the girls from the back before Riley locked everything up again. Someone had shoveled all the sidewalks and plowed the roads earlier, making it easier to get around, which was good. The last thing they needed was someone breaking a limb.

"Hey, girl!" One of the workmen near the flatbed came over to give Riley's shoulders a squeeze. "How you doin'?"

Riley laughed, her pretty smile lighting up the overcast day. Sam found himself wishing he could see that smile more often before he remembered he shouldn't. He wasn't here to admire Riley. He was here to find gifts for his daughter for Christmas. That was all.

"Sam, meet Eric Barnes," Riley said, introducing them. "We went to school together."

Sam shook the man's hand. "Seems like everyone knows everyone else around here."

"Ain't that the truth," Eric chuckled good-naturedly. "Born in Wyckford, stay in Wyckford."

"For better or worse," Riley muttered, rolling her eyes. "How's the tree coming along?"

"Good. The crane operator should be here soon and then we just need to get this puppy upright before we can decorate it in time for the pop-up festival."

"And when is that again?" Riley asked, innocent as could be.

Eric shook his head. "Nice try, Doc. You know I can't tell you that."

"What about Santa?" Ivy interrupted. "Is he coming too?"

"He'll be here for Christmas." Adi nudged her with an elbow. "It's too early, silly."

Sam knew nothing about trees but acted dutifully impressed by the huge conifer until they finally moved on, walking farther down Wyckford's main street. Along the way, Riley pointed out different spots where holiday events might take place during the festival and where Sam might find gifts for Ivy and Hala. The girls walked ahead of them, whispering excitedly about their fish costumes and what they wanted for Christmas and who knew what else. Every so often they'd look back at Sam and Riley, giggle, then go back to whispering again.

Sam was suspicious. "What do you think they're planning?"

"Who knows," Riley said, shrugging. "Let's stop at the hardware store."

"I doubt there's anything in there my daughter would want," Sam said.

"You never know," Riley countered, stopping near an elderly man in a Santa hat on a ladder outside the entrance. He was stringing up twinkle lights around the front windows. Riley frowned up at him. "Be careful, Arthur. I don't want to see you in my department again for X-rays."

Mr. Schmidt, the store's owner, glanced down at Riley. Sam had already met the man on his forays into the place for supplies to fix things around his rental home. "Stop fussing at me, missy," Arthur said. "I'm fine. I've managed to live all ninety-two years of my life without your guidance. I think I can keep doing so just fine." Then the ladder beneath him teetered slightly, and he gripped the ledge at the top of the window for dear life. "Hold on to me, will you?"

Riley steadied the ladder with one hand. "Have you met Dr. Perkins, Arthur?"

"Sure," Schmidt said, grinning down at Sam before returning his focus to his lights. "He's in here almost every weekend. Regular Bob the Builder, this one is on the weekends. How are you, Sam? Where's Ivy?"

"On up ahead." Sam held the other side of Arthur's ladder and glanced to where the girls were peering into the display window of a local candy store called Sweeties. "And I'm good, thanks. Do you want help with those lights, Mr. Schmidt?"

"Nah. I'm done." The older man clipped in the last of the string of lights then returned to the ground, still spry for his age. Arthur dusted off his hands before squinting at them both. "What brings you both downtown today? Going to try your hand at bingo?"

"Nope." Riley hiked her thumb toward Sam. "I'm giving our newest town resident a tour."

"Ah. That's nice of you." Arthur leaned closer to Sam and dropped his voice to a stage whisper. "But take heed, Dr. Perkins. This one is salty."

"Hey! I heard that." Riley scowled at them before breaking into a grin. "Okay, yes. Maybe I am salty, but there's nothing wrong with having some attitude."

"Personally, I like a firebrand woman," Arthur said, beaming at Riley.

"You like women period, Arthur," she scoffed. "Sam, did you know Mr. Schmidt got the highest bids at the town charity auction last fall? There was a regular catfight to win a date with the town's most eligible bachelor here." Riley winked at the older man, and Arthur's chest puffed up a little.

"That's right," Arthur agreed with obvious pride. "I received the highest bid of the night. Those women at the retirement village are insatiable, I tell you. Watch out for the seasoned crowd!"

Sam smiled politely, going along with the joke

but feeling a bit like he was standing outside looking in. These people had lived their whole lives together. They were like a family, albeit a dysfunctional one. And once more, Sam's chest pinched with loneliness. He'd grown up alone, no extended family at all. Then he'd married Natalia and they'd had Ivy and become their own little unit. Now it was just him and his daughter. Hala and her husband were there too, but it wasn't quite the same. He sighed. Deep down, seeing Riley interact with the townsfolk made him secretly wish he could be a part of that too. Maybe as Ivy grew up here and he met more people, he'd relax and feel more comfortable. He tried to picture himself strolling down the street there, laughing and chatting with the person beside him. A person who looked an awful lot like Riley Turner. Afterward, they'd go home, and she'd put on those pink poodle-print pj's, and he could slowly take them off her, kissing every inch of her body slowly and sweetly until they ended up naked and in bed, limbs entwined and hearts racing.

Gah!

Sam's head snapped up, and he hoped his face wasn't as red as it felt, heat prickling up from beneath the collar of his coat. He'd promised himself he wouldn't go there today. This was not supposed to happen. He should be able to control himself around her, but it seemed all it took was one grin or laugh or wink and he was lost.

Not good. He checked his watch, floundering for something to do to distract himself. "We, uh, we should keep going, Riley. You still have a lot to show me."

After a quick goodbye to Arthur, they continued walking, the girls a short distance ahead. From somewhere close, the scent of popcorn filled the air, and Wyckford municipal workers were up on cherry pickers, stretching lights across the main street. Other than that, though, the town seemed oddly quiet for a Saturday morning. Yes, it was a small town, and the temps had dropped again last night with the snow, leaving a chilly haze in the air, but he'd still expected more traffic than this.

"Where is everyone?" Sam asked, frowning as they crossed the street.

"Bingo," Riley said. "It's a Saturday-morning hot spot, like Arthur mentioned. They have prizes."

The girls had stopped again, this time in front of a local craft shop to gawk at the beautiful handmade items on display.

"Want to go in and look around?" Riley asked them.

"Yes, please!" the girls squealed in unison.

Riley whispered to Sam once the girls were inside, "Pay attention in here. See what Ivy likes, then ask the gals to hold it for you. You can come back to get it later."

Sam nodded, following her into the shop. Hardwood floors sparkled beneath a bevy of holiday cheerfulness from the bedecked artificial trees everywhere and the Christmas music playing through the speakers overhead. They were even burning pine-scented incense somewhere, giving the air a sweet scent he associated with cozy childhood dreams.

Riley started talking to the owners about the going-on in town while his daughter and Adi perused the aisles filled with toys. Sam made polite small talk with them for a moment before turning his attention to a display of hand-knit dog hats near the register, some with reindeer antlers. He thought one might look cute on Spork and picked one out for his pooch. When he finally tuned in to the conversation between Riley and the owners again, it was in time to see Riley headed for the dressing rooms near the back of the store with one of the owners by her side and an elf costume draped across her lap.

"Where are you going?" he called after her, confused.

"Be right back," she said. "Just trying this on."

He really should've paid more attention. He could never seem to find the right balance with Riley. Either he was totally locked in, lusting after her, or completely focused elsewhere. Sighing, Sam turned around and found himself face-to-face with one of the owners, Louise Dalton. He'd operated on her brother the year before for an aneurysm. "How's Robbie?" he asked. "Still progressing?"

"Yep. He's doing great, Doc." Louise beamed at him. "You saved his life. Thank you."

Even after all these years as a neurosurgeon, it still humbled him to know he'd helped people. He saw them during the worst days of their lives and was grateful when he could make things better for them. "Glad to be of service. Tell Robbie I said hello."

"Will do, Doc," Louise said before going to help another customer.

Sam wandered over to see where Ivy and Adi were and found them near the back of the store too, admiring a winter village display complete with a train that blew steam from its tiny smokestack as it circled the base of a Christmas tree.

"Look, Daddy!" Ivy pointed. "Isn't it cool? Can we get one? Please? I love trains!"

"We have a *Star Wars* one at our house," Adi said. "My dad helped me pick it out last year. It has the cantina and all the action figures. This year he said we could get a new Luke Skywalker too, since Winnie ate the old one." She looked up at Sam, squinting. "Did you know droids don't like ice?"

"I did not know," Sam said, struggling to keep up with the ping-ponging subjects.

"I don't like ice either," Adi continued. "Ice

killed my mommy and my grandparents and hurt Aunt Riley."

Okay. More unsolicited info about Riley's past, which only made him even more curious about her, which was not helpful at all in the current situation. Especially when the dressing room door opened and Riley rolled out in what had to be the sexiest elf costume known to man, complete with a jaunty cap and a little green spandex dress that looked shrink-wrapped to her body. A body he'd only ever seen in scrubs or jeans and a sweater or those silly pink pj's, but now…

Merry son of a nutcracker…

Riley flashed him a self-deprecating smile and gestured toward her outfit, as if asking his opinion, while the owner who'd helped returned to the front counter to ring up customers. Sam wanted to say something, anything, but he found himself speechless, dumbstruck by the glory that was Riley Turner in that costume. She must've taken his silence as a negative, however, because her bright smile dimmed, and she swiveled her chair back toward the dressing room again. "Never mind. I'll change."

"Wait!" Sam managed to force out before it was too late. He shook his head to clear it of the crazy image of him picking Riley up like Santa's bag of gifts, slinging her over his shoulder, and carrying her away to unwrap that green spandex from her one inch at a time, making sure to worship every inch of her until she begged for more.

She stopped, turning slightly to see him, her expression wary.

Say something, idiot!

"You look…"

Amazing? Adorable? Stunningly hot?

Sam's usually ordered mind tripped over words until what ended up coming out was "Green."

"Green?" She raised one dark brow. "Is that good or bad?"

"Good!" the girls shouted in unison.

Sam swallowed hard and nodded, saying more quietly, "Definitely good."

Riley's grin slowly returned like the sun coming out from behind snow clouds as she rolled back up to him, her other clothes and coat folded neatly in her lap. "All right then. Let's go."

It took Sam's hormone-befuddled brain a few seconds to hoist itself out of the smutty pool it had fallen into and back to reality, then he chased after her, rounding up the girls and following Riley outside. "Go where? And are you sure you don't want to change first? Won't you be cold in that?"

"No. We're just going to the end of this block. Louise said someone who helps run the bingo game called in sick, and they need extra help until lunch. Since we're already here, I told her I'd do it. Costumes are mandatory for those running

the show since the holiday season is upon us. I'll
help up front while you play bingo with the girls.
Get the whole Wyckford experience. It'll be fun."

"Bingo," Sam parroted before hurrying after
her and the girls toward a brick building on the
corner. Spending a few hours in a crowded hall
with strangers sounded like torture. As did having to keep himself from drooling over Riley in
that costume. He tried to remind himself of all
the reasons he didn't want to want her. Coworkers. Failure. Grief. Guilt. Right now, none of them
were working. Man, he was in danger here. "But
I thought we were going to look at more shops."

"I've shown you basically all of them. It's a
small town. The selection is limited if you want
to buy local. There might be some other vendors
at the pop-up festival though. Come on, Sam.
Have a little adventure."

Sam and adventure went together about as well
as turpentine and Toblerone and he felt completely out of his depth, but with the rest of them
already at the entrance to the crowded establish-
ment, and the fact they'd ridden here with Riley,
he didn't have much choice.

Before coming to Wyckford, Sam had always
considered himself a man who could handle anything, but here, now, he felt out of his league and
not ready for any of this. Not for bingo. And certainly not for his sudden, uncontrollable, ever-
increasing attraction to Riley. When she opened

the door for him, her movements showed off her bust in that costume to dazzling effect, and Sam found his resistance crumbling as he went inside with the girls.

CHAPTER SIX

THE CITIZENS OF Wyckford took their bingo seriously. What Riley hadn't expected, though, was single dad Sam's effect on the women present. Females seemed to come out of the woodwork to bring him drinks or snacks or ask if he needed help or to tell him what a great job he was doing with Ivy. It was like a man with a kid was the world's greatest aphrodisiac. Maybe it was, because even Riley had to admit he looked adorable sandwiched between the girls, showing them how to mark numbers on their cards using the pink sparkly daubers they'd insisted he get for them from the registration table. From his serious expression, he was trying to follow all the rules and proper sportsmanship in the game. Ever logical, by the book and straitlaced, that was Sam.

It would be nice to see Sam ruffled. Sexy too. *Whoops.*

No, no, no. Riley refused to melt over him. She didn't melt over men. Never had, never would.

Then he looked up and caught her eye, and the

world faded away again until it was just the two of them and no one else and...

What was up with that?

And okay, fine. Maybe there was a little melting taking place inside her.

Still, she shook it off, reminding herself she did not want a man right now. She'd worked hard for her independence and refused to give it up for anyone. Certainly not a man who hadn't even shown the least bit of interest in her. Sam always appeared cool, confident, competent and in control. Everything you wanted in a neurosurgeon.

Then she remembered how he'd blocked the elevator at the hospital the other day, fumbling his words as he asked her to come with him today. Also, just now, when she'd come out of the dressing room, he'd looked astonished at her appearance. Astonished and appreciative. It had been a while, but she still remembered what masculine interest looked and felt like. Sam had wanted her back in that store, even if he'd quickly denied it. Huh. Both times, he'd given her a peek underneath his normally stoic exterior, and she'd seen a man who was a little awkward in new social situations, who blushed under scrutiny, who obviously cared for his daughter and those around him and wanted to do what he could to support the new town he called home by buying local. It was almost enough to thaw the icy walls she'd built around her heart after the accident.

She glanced over at him again to find Lucille and her blue-haired posse from the retirement home now closing wagons around him at the table. Poor guy. From where Riley sat at the caller's table at the front of the room, she gave Sam a thumbs-up for reassurance. He flashed her a grateful grin that had her insides quivering.

Oh, boy.

Before she could anxiety spiral too much about her reactions to him though, Ben Murphy took the seat beside Riley. He was the bingo committee chair and MC that morning. He grinned and patted her shoulder. "Thanks for filling in. It's a huge help."

"Thanks. And no problem." Riley was glad for something else to focus on besides Sam and his too-attractive face. "What do you need me to do?"

"You'll be our caller this morning," Ben said. "The computer there selects the numbers. When it pops up on the screen, you call it into the mic here. We also flash them on a big screen, but the software handles all that. And don't forget to play to the crowd. The more fun they have, the more cards they buy and the more money we make for charity."

"Got it." She positioned her wheelchair next to the ball machine and proceeded to run the game for the next three hours, during which they gave away five hundred dollars in cash, two microwaves and a weekend trip for two to a casino in Boston. The octogenarian crowd was rowdy, even more than Riley expected and she was well-versed in the escapades of the residents of Sunny Village Retirement Home. At one point, she leaned over to Ben and said, "I thought they'd get tired after a while."

Ben laughed. "Not with cash and prizes up for grabs. They can go all day if it means winning."

Riley understood that all too well. She'd once camped outside the entrance to Gillette Stadium for three days to get tickets to a concert she didn't even want to see just to prove all the people who'd said she couldn't wrong.

Same with her walking again now. She'd do it, no matter what.

By the time the morning game session finally ended, it was lunchtime, and Riley was starving. She'd grabbed a quick piece of toast and coffee at Brock's earlier before picking up Sam and Ivy but nothing since. And while there'd been trays of assorted rolls and cookies passed around the game tables, she'd been too busy calling numbers to grab any. Now, as she made her way over to where Sam and their girls still sat as the rest of the crowd filed out of the building, she grabbed a remaining Danish and shoved it into her mouth to quiet her rumbling stomach. Cherry. Her favorite.

"How did it go?" she asked the girls as they left the bingo hall. It had been stuffy inside, but

Riley shivered in the cold breeze, regretting not putting her coat back on. Sam, ever the gentleman, helped her put it on while they waited for the light to change. She didn't even mind his assistance. "Did you win anything?"

"They let me keep my doober!" Ivy shouted, holding up a bright pink bottle of glitter ink.

"Dauber." Adi nudged her friend in the side before showing off her own purple glitter bottle. "Bingo!"

The conversation then descended into chaos as the girls each shouted "bingo" over and over, trying to outdo the other as they walked back toward her SUV.

"You did well," Sam said, shaking his head and smiling at his daughter's antics. "I think you missed your destiny as number caller."

"Yeah?" Riley snorted. "Maybe I'll take it up as a side hustle. Make a little extra bank for my new home nest egg." The light turned green, and they crossed the street with the rest of the group waiting around them. The overcast sky was a little brighter now, but the wind had picked up too. Halfway through the crosswalk, a piece of her hair came loose from her ponytail and blew into her face, covering her eyes. Normally it wouldn't be a problem, but Riley needed both hands for her chair. Great. She stopped, since she couldn't see anything anyway, and reached up to brush the hair away before the light turned yellow, but Sam beat her to it.

"Here," he said, his warm fingertips lingering against her skin, sending hot tingles of awareness through Riley again and making her breath catch. Time seemed to slow again, and the rest of the world faded. All she could see were his lips, his dark eyes, all she wanted was for him to kiss her, and…

A car horn beeped because they were blocking traffic. Reality snapped back to normal speed again.

Yikes.

Riley hurried toward the opposite sidewalk, Sam at her side. He seemed to take a sudden interest in anything that wasn't her. Which was fine because Riley felt like a mess inside. Why was she acting like this around him? She didn't want to be involved with him, regardless of how attracted to Sam she was. It seemed to take forever to reach the SUV, even though it was only two blocks away. Finally, they got to her vehicle and Sam helped the girls into the back while Riley got herself situated behind the wheel once more. After starting the engine, she fiddled with the radio as he buckled himself into his seat belt in the passenger seat.

They drove away, circling the block to head back toward Sam's place. To fill the awkward

TRACI DOUGLASS   95

void, Riley said, "Thanks for being a good sport about the bingo."

"Thanks for showing me around town," he countered, staring out the window beside him instead of at her. Just as well, because Riley didn't trust herself not to throw herself into his arms at this point. She needed time alone to sort through all this and figure out what was happening here. "We've been in Wyckford over a year now, but I don't think I've ever experienced this place in the same way I did today. I'm grateful to you for showing me that."

Her insides warmed despite the lingering chill inside the car. Sam Perkins seemed to push all her buttons when it came to wanting. Made her feel things she hadn't since the accident. Heady stuff. Scary stuff too, and she wasn't sure what to do with it. It had come out of nowhere. What was also strange, and dangerous, was how she kept forgetting about everything else—the accident, the cold, the girls, her vow to stand on her own two feet, everything—all of it zeroing down to only him whenever their gazes locked, or he touched her. Riley was used to being the person who seduced, not the other way around. They drove back to his house on autopilot, her mind racing as she pulled into his driveway without even realizing they'd arrived.

Ivy and Adi clambered out of the car on their own and entered the house using the security keypad on the front door let themselves in, while Riley and Sam watched from the SUV. Neither of them moved until Riley couldn't stand it anymore. "I guess I'll see you—"

Before she could finish that sentence, however, Sam kissed her, soft and slow. Stunned, Riley froze before relaxing into it. He felt warm and solid and infinitely sweet, and something tightly coiled and stiff inside her unfurled, softened. His warmth, the softness of his lips, the way his hands cupped her cheeks like she was precious and fleeting and infinitely desirable made her want to burrow into him and stay there forever...

Finally, after a long, breathless moment, Sam pulled away, looking as shocked as Riley felt. His dark eyes fathomless and voice low, he muttered, "I'm not sure why I did that. I just...there's something about you...something... I can't seem to..."

Still mumbling, he got out and went inside, sending Adi back to Riley few moments later.

Nonplused, she drove home, silent while her niece continued to chatter about bingo.

Sam had officially lost his mind. That was the only explanation he could come up with for why he'd kissed Riley. One second, he'd been reminding himself about all the reasons he should leave her alone, and the next, his logical mind had taken a back seat to his libido. All he'd been able to see was Riley's little green dress and her big blue eyes and how he'd like to slide his hand up her thigh, to see if he could make her blush again, and...

Man, he was in trouble here.

Bemused, he hung up their coats then headed for the kitchen to pull something from the freezer to defrost for later while his daughter went upstairs to her room to play. Sam did his best to shake off the lingering sensual haze clouding his brain after their encounter. It was so strange, the sudden lust that seemed to overtake his common sense whenever he was around Riley now. What had changed? What had inexplicably made him veer off his chosen path of being alone, of focusing on his work and raising his daughter? He didn't *want* to want her, and yet he did.

The most frustrating part for him though was that the awareness, the attraction to her went beyond just the physical. He cared about what she thought, enjoyed talking to her, loved her intelligence and sharp wit. And it all seemed completely out of his control, which was a real problem for him on so many levels. He didn't get involved with colleagues, especially ones who were so incredibly, inconveniently mesmerizing to him. But there was no denying their chemistry now. His lips still tingled from their kiss. He licked them and tasted her there. Sugar and mint and a hint of cherry.

Gah! He needed this gone. Right now.

He couldn't let Riley into his life. He couldn't protect her. Least of all from himself.

Sam mentally scolded himself as he got a glass of water then checked his emails at the counter. The best way to stop it was to go cold turkey, like a drug. That kiss would not be repeated. Sam wasn't looking for more than a professional relationship with anyone. He'd been there, done that, failed spectacularly and had the shattered heart to prove it.

Still, his curiosity about Riley remained. He wanted to know more about her. Everything about her.

Which was not possible because they wouldn't be seeing each other again outside of work. Speaking of work, he decided to talk to Riley on Monday at the hospital and confront the issue head-on, explain that the kiss had been a mistake. One they wouldn't repeat. He couldn't imagine her arguing since she didn't like him that way either.

Does she?

Yes, she'd responded beautifully to his kiss, but that could've just been the shock of it all.

Frustrated now in more ways than one, Sam strode into the living room, determined to settle things once and for all. None of this was real. It couldn't be. No one was lovestruck like that outside of cheesy romance movies. The holidays were always a stressful time and both he and

Riley were overworked, which would explain it. They were both probably looking for an easy outlet for all that tension. Once January rolled around, all this would go away. Whatever *this* was. Until then, they'd avoid each other outside of work as much as possible. Problem solved.

Spork jumped up onto the couch beside him, dropping his octopus stuffie into Sam's lap before flopping over onto his back, legs in the air and tongue lolling out of the side of his mouth in a goofy doggo grin as he presented his belly for rubs. Sam snorted and shook his head. Oh, to be a dog, where everything was so clear, and the most important thing was having a good toy and good treats. Spork wanted affection, so he asked for it. End of story.

Emotions were what caused the problems, Sam decided. They turned minor diversions into major crises.

Which only proved his theory that they were best kept locked away so they couldn't make trouble.

Compartmentalizing was proving easier said than done though, because every time Sam closed his eyes, he imagined he could still smell Riley's cinnamon scent, still feel the softness of her cheek when he'd brushed the hair from her face, still hear the catch in her breath as she'd relaxed into his kiss...

He scrubbed a hand over his face. If he was

honest with himself—which he seemed determined not to be—what worried him the most was all these messy feelings swirling deep inside him were ones he'd thought were long buried. The yearning for intimacy, the sense of breathless passion, the connection and care. He didn't have the time or the energy to deal with this anymore.

Sam sighed and stared at the wall across from him. Thank goodness he had Sunday off to recover. He could rest and recharge and sort all this out once and for all. Put it all in proper perspective before talking with Riley on Monday.

He started to relax. It would be all right.

Then his phone buzzed, and he peered down at his screen, expecting to see an alert or update from the hospital about one of his patients. Instead, he saw a text from Riley.

We need to talk.

She was correct, but that didn't stop the muscles in Sam's upper back from knotting.

He opened his messenger app and saw three bouncing dots then a new message.

Do you have time tomorrow?

He'd planned to push their conversation to Monday, but maybe it was better to get it over

with sooner rather than later. So, he texted back,
asking her when and where.

One thirty tomorrow. Meet in Radiology.

Sam took a deep breath then confirmed. Afterward, he messaged Hala to see if she could watch
Ivy for a few hours the next day before leaning
back against the couch cushions, torn between
laughing and locking himself away until this all
disappeared.

He loved the peaceful, ordered life he'd built
for himself and Ivy. He could keep her safe here.

The chaos Riley caused inside him didn't seem
compatible with that at all.

CHAPTER SEVEN

AT THE APPOINTED time on Sunday afternoon, Riley sat across from Sam in the reading room, doing her best not to notice how his biceps bulged enticingly beneath the soft-looking black sweater he wore. A muscle was ticking near his jaw again too, the one that went to town when he was irritated, or stressed, or both. When had she noticed that about him? It didn't matter. What mattered was after today, she wouldn't notice it anymore. He must be having second thoughts about their kiss too, right? That should make her feel better, that they were both on the same page. For some odd reason, it didn't.

All she knew for certain was this situation was banana pants stressful, and she wanted it over with.

She wanted to go back to her independent lifestyle where the only person she thought about 24/7 was herself. Not in a selfish way—in a put-your-own-oxygen-mask-on-first way. Instead, right now, Sam had seemed to infiltrate her every waking moment. Her every sleeping moment too, if the way she'd woken up in a sweat this morning—to images from her dreams of them together, naked and tangled in her sheets, limbs entwined—was any indication...

Lord, she was in a bad way here. And that wasn't good.

"Look, I'm sorry about what happened yesterday, this kiss," Sam said, finally. "I never should have done that."

Riley shrugged, nodding slightly. "It was unexpected, that's for sure."

"I don't even know why it happened." He dropped his head and rubbed the back of his neck. "I was ready to say goodbye...and then..." He sighed and closed his eyes. "It doesn't matter why it happened. It was inappropriate, and I'm sorry."

"Okay," she said agreeably, though she was feeling anything but. She felt cold and lost inside, unsure what was going on and why, but just knowing she had to make it through this or else everything would change, and everything had already changed so much, and she wasn't sure how much she could take anymore.

He looked up at her response, his eyes narrowed. "That's it? That's all you have to say? 'Okay'?"

Confused, she frowned. "Do you want to fight about it?"

"No." He shook his head and looked away

again. "I just want to make sure it doesn't happen again."

"It was a kiss, Sam, not rocket science. Sometimes people just do things spontaneously." Seeing him so discombobulated about it made her wonder if he'd ever done a single unexpected thing in his life. And sure, it *had* been a mistake, but that didn't mean it hadn't been good. Better than good. It'd knocked her socks off in a way that hadn't occurred in years, but Riley wasn't going to flip out about it. "Living outside the everyday can be fun."

"It can also be dangerous. No, thank you. I like control, order, logic."

"I know," she said, her tone not exactly flattering.

"Like that's a bad thing," Sam grumbled. "Control keeps us safe."

"It also keeps us locked in a cage. And that's just sad."

"Sad how?" Sam scowled at her from across the room. "In my experience, acting recklessly only makes people less safe."

Well, she couldn't argue there. Sitting there in a wheelchair, she was living proof.

The knowledge didn't make her feel any better. In fact, it only made her angrier. She didn't want to catch feels for Sam Perkins. Didn't want to moon over him and his biceps. Riley did *not* moon over men. From the age of sixteen, she'd dated lots of guys. Rebels, bad boys, hot guys, cool guys, cute guys, nerdy guys, and in one unfortunate case, an actual criminal. But in all those encounters, she'd been the one making the choices, the one with the power in the relationship.

Sam and her stupid attraction to him had turned the tables on her though. It wasn't just the fact that he was hot and nerdy and ticked a lot of boxes she was looking for with his smarts and his strength. She also sensed a deep well of pain and emotions that drew her in and made her want to help him, heal him, and that was like poison to her freedom. The longer she let this go on, the greater the risk she'd fall for him even more—she'd always been a sucker for wounded heroes—and then she'd end up *needing* him and not just wanting him and… Her sense of self-preservation kicked in and she rushed to offer, "How about we just agree to forget it completely and move forward as professional colleagues? Nothing more."

Sam looked pleased by that potential solution, but before he could respond, an alarm went off in the corridor indicating a Code Blue, meaning a patient had gone into cardiac arrest, had respiratory problems, or another type of medical emergency on the floor. Not uncommon in Radiology, since many of the patients they saw were to diagnose the cause of serious to life-threatening conditions sent from the ER. All the staff were trained to respond, including Riley and Sam. Without hesitation, they both hurried out of the reading room, heading toward a treatment room at the end of the hall where a blue light flashed above the door. Inside, they found a middle-aged man on an exam table, the top of his hospital gown open to reveal his chest as someone performed CPR. Riley rolled in and checked the patient's airway before grabbing an Ambu bag to administer oxygen to the patient as Sam took over chest compressions from the bedside nurse.

"Status?" he asked.

The charge nurse, who stood near a screen in the corner, read from the patient's digital chart. "Sixty-two-year-old male, admitted last night in preparation for a laparoscopic surgery today. He was brought here an hour ago for preliminary ultrasounds, then began having trouble breathing. His systolic blood pressure dropped to the low eighties. No history of heart problems. We shocked him at one fifty for a V-fib arrest a minute and a half ago before you arrived. Patient is still in V-fib."

"Thanks," Sam said. "Any meds given yet?"

"No," the charge nurse said. "We do have IV access."

"Let's give epi then," Sam said.

Riley didn't interrupt, since closed-loop communication was critical during a Code Blue. Too many people giving orders only confused the situation and risked the patient's life even more. At the next pulse check, they all rotated positions. The bedside nurse took over the Ambu bag for Riley, and Riley moved to the digital chart on the wall, while a radiology tech took over compressions for Sam. Sam moved to check the monitors and the defibrillator machine, which was charging again on the counter nearby.

"One milligram of epi in," the charge nurse said.

"Good." Sam stepped in beside Riley to see the man's chart the check the man's vitals again. "Good airway and ventilation but he's still in V-fib. Let's go ahead and shock again. Charging at two hundred joules." When a sharp, high-pitched beep sounded, he said, "Everybody stand clear." Once everyone had moved away from the patient, he pressed the large red button on the machine. The patient's body convulsed quickly. "Shock delivered. Resume CPR."

"Resuming compressions," the radiology tech said. "Ten seconds to pulse check."

At the ten-second mark, Sam took the patient's carotid pulse. "He has a pulse."

"Hold compressions," the charge nurse said.

"God job, everyone," Sam said. "Let's secure the airway and call ICU."

Once the team from intensive care arrived, and

they'd successfully made the handoff, Riley and Sam went back out into the hall.

Instead of heading for the reading room again, however, Riley went for the elevators, pressing the down button. "I don't know about you, but I could use some fresh air."

Sam followed. "Me too."

They rode down to the first floor in silence, both seemingly lost in their thoughts as they proceeded through the lobby to a side plaza area. It was mid-December now, so the tables set up there for lunchtime during the spring and summer were stacked neatly against the wall, awaiting warmer weather again. Their breath frosted on the air, but at least Riley had dressed more appropriately than he had today, with a thick sweater and pants beneath her lab coat. Sam only had on his cashmere turtleneck and jeans. He'd left his jacket upstairs. His mind kept flashing back to the tiny green elf costume though, and his fantasies of stripping it off Riley, but he hoped the cold and the lingering adrenaline rush from the code upstairs would shove those errant thoughts firmly away as they stood alone near the center of the courtyard.

Riley said, "Did you know there's a legend about this fountain? They say if you stand before the water and wish for true love with a true heart, it'll happen for you."

Sam snorted. He'd never taken her for a sappy

romantic, but he must've been wrong because Riley arched a brow at him. "It's empty now. What does that mean?"

"No clue," she asked, her tone pointed. "Probably that we're a couple of losers."

"Perfect." He tucked his hands into his pockets to keep them warm. "I never took you for someone who bought into legends and myths."

"You think love is a myth?" Riley gave him some side-eye. "You were married."

Sam's chest pinched a little. He did not want to go there, but he'd walked right into that. "Yes. I was. And I loved Natalia more than my life. And now she's gone."

Riley exhaled slowly. "I'm sorry for your loss."

"Thank you."

She stared at the fountain again. "Is that why you keep to yourself so much?"

"Yes." He shrugged. "I want to protect myself and those I care for. Can't do that if I'm vulnerable, so I've conditioned myself to not get invested emotionally past a certain level. Like you have."

Riley gave him an incredulous expression, her salty side coming out in full force as she used air quotes for emphasis. "What do you mean 'like me'?"

"You keep to yourself as well. We've worked together off and on for a year now," he said, "and I've never seen you with anyone. Don't deny it."

She looked back at the fountain, clearly hat-ing that she'd been that obvious and that he'd noticed. Several tense seconds ticked by before she answered, low enough that he would've missed it if he hadn't been watching her so closely. "No. You're not wrong."

"Riley!" someone called then, interrupting them.

It was Luna Norton, a physical therapist at the hospital. Sam had met her a few times, mainly at the diner she worked at that was owned by her parents. There were only two restaurants in town and one of them was also a bar, so when he and Ivy went out to eat, they went to the Buzzy Bird. Mark Bates was with her. Sam had met him briefly at the diner. He seemed nice enough, and completely besotted with Luna, poor man. "Hey, Dr. Perkins," Luna said to Sam as she reached them, but her attention was fixed on Riley. "Are you working today too?"

"I am." Riley smiled. "Just finished a code upstairs, so came down for a quick break. Why?"

"No reason." Luna's curious gaze darted between Riley and Sam, then fixed on Sam for a long beat, a warning in her eyes that Sam understood immediately because he'd used it himself where his daughter was concerned.

Hurt her and you'll die slowly and painfully.

Right. Sam shuffled his feet to maintain circulation in his chilled toes, wondering why Luna felt the need to warn him about Riley. They weren't involved nor would they be. That was the whole point of today. Which reminded him…

Once Luna and Mark went back inside, and Sam and Riley were alone again, he ignored the pinch of regret in his chest and said, "I accept your offer."

"Huh?" Riley squinted up at him.

"What you said upstairs. We forget about the kiss and move forward as professional colleagues only. I agree that's the best way."

"Oh." She stared into the frozen fountain again. "Okay."

And just like that, it was over. He should be happy. Thrilled. Except he felt…*disappointed.*

Sam scrambled to figure out why as his analytical brain popped up facts like a scoreboard. Fact one: he'd kissed Riley. Fact two: she'd kissed him back. Fact three: that kiss had been the best thing to happen to him in recent memory, and now all Sam could seem to think about was doing it again, even though that was the absolute worst idea in modern history.

And that's exactly why he had to stick with this arrangement, for better or worse.

Sam sighed and pinched the bridge of his nose as they went back upstairs. In the reading room, Riley kept her attention firmly on the file in front of her, which was good because Sam didn't think he could get through this with those pretty blue eyes watching him. He should leave. He wanted to leave. But then he sat down again and asked, "Why do you use a wheelchair?"

Riley, still salty apparently, snapped at him over her shoulder. "Because I like the aesthetic. Why do you think?"

Yeah, he'd misphrased that question and now felt worse than before. *Idiot.* "I'm sorry."

Riley shot him a sour glare. "Look, why are you still here? We made a deal. The kiss is forgotten, okay? Leave me alone. It's fine. I'm fine."

"You're clearly not fine," he said quietly before he could stop himself.

She opened her mouth, closed it, then opened it again. "Not your problem, okay? I am not yours to fix."

Sam sat forward and scrubbed his hands over his face. "I don't want to fix you, Riley. I think you're great as you are. Better than great. Amazing."

Several long moments passed before Riley finally turned to face him, her expression guarded, and her gaze lowered as she said, "I was in a car accident. The car lost control on the ice and skidded into the bay. My parents died instantly. I broke my back in three places and had spinal cord damage. That's why I use the chair. The accident was my fault. They were only out that night because of me."

"I'm so sorry." He sat back, exhaling slowly. "Thank you for sharing that with me."

Riley nodded, looking up at him at last. "How did your wife die?"

"She was diagnosed with ALS at thirty-four and passed away two years ago, before I could find a cure for her. I failed my wife. I won't fail my patients."

They sat across from each other then, silent, as a new understanding hung heavy between them. Part of him was glad Riley had finally confided in him, but instead of quenching his curiosity about her, it only made him want to know more. Why did she feel responsible? He was sure that wasn't the case, but before he could ask more, his phone buzzed. He checked his screen and winced. "I've got to get home to Ivy. Hala needs to leave soon."

"Right." Riley turned back around to face her desk, her face flushed and her eyes damp. "Guess I'll see you on the next case then."

Sam stood, reluctant to leave after what they'd shared, despite their agreement. He pulled on his jacket and started for the door, unsure what to say to make things better between them. She stopped him before he reached the hall. "And, Sam? Thanks for telling me about your wife."

He gave a slow nod. "Thanks for telling me about your accident."

Then he walked away, that dreaded warmth in his chest toward her blossoming anew, telling him that his emotions were still involved where Riley was concerned, regardless of their deal. That spelled big, big trouble, because if he couldn't stop those emotions from spreading to his heart then all bets were off.

CHAPTER EIGHT

"THIS IS A TERRIFIC HOUSE, Riley. One of my favorites in the area. And it's close to your brother's place as well," Lynette Thompson, the Realtor, said as she led her into a nice ranch-style home with bay access. "It's been newly remodeled within the last three years, though I can see a few areas where accessibility might be a problem for you. The entrance out front, for instance, and the higher kitchen island and counters, out of reach for someone using a wheelchair or a scooter. All easily fixable by a licensed contractor though."

Riley looked around, taking in the crisp white trim and hardwood floors. She liked the contemporary style and the updated conveniences, such as the quartz countertops in the kitchen. "Can we look at the rest?"

"Sure thing." Lynette handed Riley a spec sheet on the property before leading her around from room to room for the next half an hour, ending with a large master bedroom and attached bathroom. The house was graceful and lovely, though it had been built in a different era without any thought toward accommodating those with mobility challenges. Still, Riley could envision how much better it could work for her with a few updates.

"It's four bedrooms, two and a half baths, so plenty of room for guests. Built in 1958 and sits on a third-of-an-acre waterfront lot. You're just a short distance away from the private beach and have picturesque views from your back patio year-round. There's even a boardwalk that leads from your patio down to the water. And with lots of windows and glass doors overlooking Buzzards Bay, it makes the indoor and outdoor living seamless. As I said, with a few modifications, I think it could work well for you."

"Hmm." Riley was already doing calculations in her head. She'd prequalified for a mortgage through her local lender, knowing how cutthroat the current housing market was, but she also wanted to bring a contractor through before signing on the dotted line to make sure all the necessary changes could be done within her budget. Trouble was, she'd been so busy lately, she hadn't had time to find anyone to do the work yet. "I think so too, but I'd like a second opinion first before I move forward. How quickly do you need my answer?"

"As quickly as possible, unfortunately," Lynette said. "You know how fast properties go around here. I'll hold other buyers off as long as I can, but I really need to know before Christmas, which gives you two weeks. The current owners want this done soon so they can enjoy their retirement in Florida."

"Okay." Riley pulled out her phone to make notes on her next steps. "I'll find a contractor ASAP then schedule another tour through the property with them. Thanks, Lynette."

"Sure thing, hon." The Realtor led her back toward the entrance and out to the brick front walk. Riley's vehicle was parked in the nice driveway beside the house, in front of an attached two-car garage. The neighbors were busy shoveling the sidewalks in front of their houses, lit by moonlight, the streetlamps and the glow from all the colorful Christmas lights in yards even though it was only 5:00 p.m.

"We'll talk soon," Lynette said.

"We will." Riley waved, then got back into her car to head home to pick up Adi. Today they'd announced in the media the grand opening of the long-awaited Ice, Ice Baby pop-up festival downtown, and she'd somehow lucked out and had the evening off. She'd promised her niece earlier that once the festival opened, they'd go, since Brock and Cassie were both stuck at the hospital a lot lately. As she drove through town, crowds were already filling the area, especially around the town square, which had been blocked off for all the vendors and the ice rink. For the first time that year, it felt like the holidays were coming.

But as she passed the building where she and Sam and the girls had played bingo the week prior, her spirits sank. She and Sam hadn't seen each other much since their talk in the reading room. He hadn't even had any cases on her docket this week, which was odd. Riley wasn't sure if he'd done that on purpose to avoid her or if fate had intervened, but either way, it didn't matter. They'd made the right decision putting an end to things after that kiss. Neither of them needed or wanted the complication. They were both just getting their lives back on track after trauma. No reason to screw it up now with messy emotional entanglements that may or may not last.

Not even ones as hot as Sam Perkins.

Adi was waiting impatiently for her when she arrived at her brother's house. Riley barely had a chance to go inside and change out of her scrubs and into regular clothes before her young niece all but tugged her out the door again to go to the festival. Riley at least made sure Winnie, a potty break outside, was locked safely in her pen with food and water before heading back downtown.

Sam didn't want to be here.

But as he weaved through the crowded town square, following his daughter from the parking lot toward the temporary ice rink, he knew there was no backing out. Ivy had been talking about nothing but Ice, Ice Baby for weeks, and Sam couldn't let her down, regardless of the fact he'd had less than ten hours sleep total this week due to being on call, in addition to his busy regular schedule. He'd barely had time to eat, let alone sleep a full night.

"I can't wait to skate, Daddy," Ivy called, bouncing on her toes with excitement in front of him. She glowed nearly as bright as the holiday lights around her. "Will you skate with me?"

Sam hadn't been on a rink since he'd been nine and gone on an ill-fated field trip with his school class. They'd met some hockey players—yes, they had hockey in California—and he'd had the crazy notion to impress a girl he'd liked in his class, Ida Thong. Unfortunately for Sam, he'd had no clue what he was doing and ended up making a fool of himself in front of everyone by face-planting on the ice right in front of Ida. Repeating that experience now with Ivy wasn't at the top of his to-do list, but his exhausted brain couldn't come up with a good reason to refuse, so he went with, "Maybe."

The entrance to the temporary rink was draped with strings of colored lights and ringed by crackling metal barrel fires all around the edge. Ivy stopped near a kid about her age who wore a stocking cap that had to be about eighteen inches long. She tapped them on the shoulder and the kid turned, grinning as they saw her. "Hey, Nic!" Ivy said, all but vibrating with energy. "I can't wait to ice-skate. It's my very first time!"

"You never skated before?" Nic asked, looking dubious.

Ivy shrugged. "No. Where are your parents?"

The kid pointed toward some vendor stalls nearby. "My dad isn't here, but my mom and my sisters are getting hot chocolate."

"Oh, I love hot chocolate!" Ivy rounded on Sam again. "Daddy, can we get some? Please?"

Based on the lines, Sam's first instinct was to tell his daughter they should rent skates first, before they ran out, but the words died on his lips at Ivy's eager smile. He hadn't seen her so happy since before her mom died, and he couldn't refuse. "Sure. Let's get cocoa, then we'll get in line for skates."

They headed toward the hot chocolate vendor stall, which was more of a tiny trailer that seemed too small for an adult human to stand upright in. A woman wearing antlers and a red-and-white-striped top was taking orders at the window. Sam and Ivy joined the back of a line with about six or seven people ahead of them.

While they waited, someone came up behind them in line, but Sam didn't turn around, at least not until he was tapped on the back of the leg. Then he glanced over his shoulder to find Adi

Turner grinning up at him, missing at least one tooth.

"Hi, Dr. Perkins!" she said, waving up at him before stepping around him to Ivy's side.

Riley was there too, giving him a small smile from her chair. "Fancy seeing you here."

"Yes." Sam forced himself to breathe. He hadn't seen her in several days and had managed to convince himself his reactions to her had all been in his imagination. But it seemed all it took was one encounter and he was right back to a racing heart and tight throat. To avoid making a fool of himself, he turned back around to face the trailer. "Ivy is very excited to skate for the first time."

"Adi too, though this isn't her first time," Riley said, apparently unaffected by seeing him again. "She takes lessons. The festival's always a good time though. Everyone in town gets into the spirit. Never feels like Christmas to me until the ice rink is open."

Sam had to admit it was a jolly scene, with all those colorful lights, Christmas music coming from a live band playing on a makeshift stage set up on one side of the area, and those flames flickering in the night.

The line finally moved forward and the people in front of Sam reached the window, where they ordered ten hot chocolates. Either they had a serious cocoa addiction or they were part of a group. This would probably take forever. Just his luck.

Riley peered around him at the window then settled back in her chair, apparently coming to terms with waiting a while as she asked, "What holiday traditions did you have in California?"

"Natalia always handled it." The familiar sting of loss he felt when bringing up his wife had dulled, less like a sharp jab and more like a vague ache. Huh. That was new. "Most years we'd take off the week between Christmas and New Year's to spend a few days at the beach with Ivy."

"Sounds nice," Riley said, her tone tinged with a sadness that tugged at Sam's heart. "The holidays are tough when you're missing someone."

"True." Sam corralled the girls to keep them in line in front of him. "But I'm determined to make this Christmas special for Ivy. New town. New traditions. New memories."

"You're making a good start of it," Riley said, surprising him enough that he turned around again to look at her. Her blue eyes sparkled, and his pulse tripped. Sam tried to tell himself it was just the cold December night and his exhaustion, but even he had to admit that with the snow lightly falling and the laughter and joy all around, the night suddenly seemed more magical.

"Next!" the reindeer at the window called and Sam stepped forward. "May I help you?"

"Four hot cocoas, please, with marshmallows and extra whipped cream."

"Right away, sir."

"You don't have to buy us hot chocolate," Riley said.

"My treat." Sam handed his card to the woman in the trailer, where another antler-bedecked reindeer bustled around behind her preparing his drinks, inserting the filled cups into a cardboard drink holder, then sliding it all out the window toward him. He tucked his card and wallet safely away again before picking it up the tray, along with some napkins, then turning to face the girls and Riley. "Let's find a table to sit down before I spill these all over myself or someone else."

They worked their way back through the crowd toward the rink, crossing some bumpy snow and icy sidewalks. It couldn't have been a smooth ride for Riley under the best of circumstances, and Sam was impressed with her ability to handle her chair. He told her as much.

Riley glanced up at him, smiling. "Thanks. I switched last year to an upgraded model that's more all-terrain, plus it has a power assist motor if I need help over grass or gravel."

"Which you're probably too stubborn to use," he added, not looking at her. He wasn't flirting. Nope. This was just small talk, no matter how enjoyable bantering with her was. He suddenly didn't want to leave now. In fact, he wanted to spend as much time as possible with the sweet scent of cocoa wafting around him and a gorgeous woman at his side.

"You know me so well," Riley said, shooting him a quick wink, which made Sam stop in his tracks.

He battled a sudden wild urge to toss the drink holder into the snow and pull Riley into his arms and kiss her silly instead. Which would be a direct violation of their agreement. Instead, he turned abruptly and headed for the first open table he saw, calling behind him as he prayed for more willpower to get through this night unscathed. "This way."

Riley wasn't sure exactly what was happening, but Sam's abrupt shift in mood bothered her. Yes, they had an agreement, but that didn't mean they couldn't be cordial to each other, at least in public. When they'd been waiting in line, he'd been charming enough, and he'd even bought them all hot chocolate. For a crazy second, it had felt like *something*.

But, of course, it wasn't. Sam had made it clear he wasn't looking for romance, and neither was she. She had too much going on already, with work and her new house hunt. She didn't want him that way anyway. Even if the sizzle in her nervous system said she did.

He led them to an empty table near the edge of

the dining area and the next few moments were a flurry of distributing drinks and throwing away the cardboard drink holder. Which was good, because it allowed Riley to make a shift of her own, from sappy to salty where Sam was concerned. She didn't try to be deliberately prickly with people, but it had become a defense mechanism since the accident. And where Sam was concerned, her heart needed all the defenses it could get.

"Thanks, Aunt Riley," Adi said, snatching her cup and taking a swig before fanning her mouth. "It's hot!"

"That's why they call it hot chocolate," Riley retorted, shaking her head. "You know that."

"We should rent skates," Sam said, eyeing the ever-growing line nearby. "We don't want them to run out."

"I have my own skates." Adi proudly patted the *Star Wars* backpack she'd brought with her. "But Ivy needs some."

"I'll go grab them," Sam said, barely glancing at Riley. "You all stay here, so we don't lose the table."

"Yes, sir." Riley gave him a mock salute, which made the girls giggle.

Twenty minutes later, Sam returned with a pair of pink rental skates for his daughter and another, larger, black pair that Riley assumed had to be for him, because she certainly couldn't skate. Sam helped Ivy with hers before putting on his own.

The girls had only finished about half of their cocoa but seemed eager to get out onto the rink.

"Can we go out now, Aunt Riley?" Adi asked.

"You'll have to ask Sam, since he's the ice king going with you," Riley told her niece. Sam looked over at her double entendre and Riley just raised a brow at him. As if it wasn't true. The man could turn his emotions off on a dime.

"Dr. Perkins is a king?" Adi asked, frowning.

"Does that make me a princess?" Ivy asked. "I've always wanted to be a princess. Like Elsa!"

Riley shook her head and chuckled at yet another ice reference.

Sam placed a hand on his daughter's shoulder while shooting Riley visual daggers. "You're always a princess to me, *yeobo*."

"Okay." Adi jumped up from the picnic table and nearly fell in her skates on the uneven ground. The indoor facility where she took lessons had nice, even floors. "I'm ready!"

Sam and Ivy stood too, both as wobbly as newborn foals. Riley's heart did a little flip despite her wishes. The man could be so darn sweet when he tried to be. Like when he'd brushed the hair from her eyes, or when he'd listened to her story about the accident and not tried to give her the usual platitudes, instead really taking it in and then thanking her for sharing...

Warmth that had nothing to do with the fire nearby blossomed and grew inside her.

"Hold on to me as we go to the rink, so we stay together," he said, taking each girl's hand, one on either side of him as they traversed the short distance to the rink entrance amidst much giggling from the girls.

They stopped just outside to take off their blade protectors and Riley found herself calling to them, "I'll be cheering you all on from here."

So much for her salty queen act.

Adi and Ivy gave her thumbs-ups while Sam just watched her warily, then all three of them staggered out to the ice, holding each other for balance. Riley had skated out there so many times herself growing up. It was bittersweet now to watch others doing what she couldn't.

Someday, she reminded herself.

She sipped her cocoa, throat aching with both sadness and determination. She would get back out there again, no matter what. When she set her mind to something, she did it. Visions of her and Sam and the girls skating together, holding hands, laughing and teasing each other, being a family filled her head before she could stop them. The intense yearning hit so hard then that she had to bat away tears. Where had that come from? Yes, she missed her old life and old dreams, but that didn't mean she wanted Sam to replace them.

Did it?

She swiftly brushed her mitten-covered hands under her eyes. No. That was ridiculous. She'd

just missed all this, that was all. Missed the cama-
raderie and fun. Missed the companionship and
support. And okay, fine—maybe she'd missed
seeing Sam the past week or so, if only in passing.
She'd gotten used to his quirkiness in her reading room, and having it gone left a void. A Sam-
shaped void. And she missed Ivy too, hanging
around at the house with Adi, giggling and playing and doing all the stuff seven-year-old girls
did. She hadn't known Sam and his daughter that
long, but they'd somehow become a part of her
life while she wasn't looking. And Sam was a
good man, even if he wasn't the man for her.

I wish he was.

Riley froze at the sudden realization, blink-
ing at the rink as the trio completed another pass
around the ice. Sam looked over at her and waved,
a wide grin splitting his handsome face, and she
found herself wondering what it would be like to
be loved by him.

Wait. What?

No way had her crazy attraction to Sam grown
into more without her knowing. How could it
have? They'd barely said two words to each other
this week, and they had an agreement. No more
kisses. No romance. No more anything beyond
the professional. That's what she'd wanted—what
she'd asked for.

But apparently her heart had other ideas.

She was still grappling with it all when the girls returned, followed closely by Sam himself.

Adi headed straight to Riley and hugged her over the side of the wheelchair, exclaiming, "That was so cool! I didn't even fall once."

"Good job!" Riley said, her eyes fixed to Sam's over the top of her niece's head. What was she going to tell him? How was she going to deal with this? The last thing she needed was him going all possessive boyfriend on her, thinking he had to help her, cure her, like he had with his wife. She didn't want that, had never wanted that. Panic had her spiraling as she pulled away from Adi.

"I wish you could come with us, Aunt Riley," her niece said, snapping Riley out of it.

"Me too," Riley mumbled as she tore her gaze away from Sam's too-perceptive one. "Maybe next year."

"Is my cocoa still hot?" Ivy asked through chattering teeth. "I'm freezing."

"It is." Riley pushed the cup over to her. "Drink up, munchkin."

"After you finish, we have to go." Sam sat down beside his daughter to change back into his shoes. "You girls have school tomorrow."

"Do we have to?" Adi and Ivy whined together.

"Afraid so," Sam said, sounding wistful, like he wished the night could continue.

Riley got it. But she had to get out of there, had to go home and think this through. What a mess.

She'd thought she and Sam had doused the fire when they'd decided to keep things professional between them. She'd thought she was safe from falling for him because she'd put him in a tidy friend box, but nope. He'd somehow escaped and now threatened to burn down all her barriers and put the future she'd thought she wanted at risk. It was all overwhelming and confusing and more than a little tantalizing, giving her new possibilities she hadn't expected before.

Distracted, she tapped Adi on the arm. "Get your boots back on too, then I'll race you back to our car."

CHAPTER NINE

"ALL RIGHT, MR. LANGSTON, your scans are done," Riley said to the older man on the CT table through the speaker system. "The tech will help you sit up when you're ready, and once you've changed, the orthopedist will talk with you in his office downstairs."

Harry Langston, the town auctioneer, fussed with the white hospital gown covering his top half, scowling through the glass at her. "He's always late. Not like you. You run a tight ship, missy."

"Dr. Warner is very busy." Riley hid her grin at the compliment. She'd known Harry since she was a girl and underneath his bluster, he was just a big softy. "Take your time then."

Still frowning, Harry allowed the tech to help him off the table and into the dressing room. Despite what he'd said about Riley running a tight ship, today, she was decidedly behind. She'd had a full schedule already, made worse by several emergencies that had needed to be worked in from the ER, including Mr. Langston, who'd hurt his back decorating the front of his auction house downtown. He'd claimed he wanted it to look nice for the extra visitors who'd come to town for the festival, but Riley suspected it was part of the ongoing rivalry between him and Arthur at the hardware store. Those two were always trying to outdo each other.

By the time Harry was finished, Riley met him in the hall.

"You're all set," she said, smiling at him. "Go on down to orthopedics on the second floor. I called them, and the nurse there is expecting you."

He gave her a repentant glance. "Sorry for my mood. My stupid phone isn't working right, even though I just got it. Won't save anything. Says my memory is full."

Riley frowned. She knew for a fact Harry had gotten his device the year before, because she'd been in the store at the same time getting hers, so it didn't sound right that it wasn't working. Harry unlocked the phone then handed it to her. She scrolled through, checking a few settings until she found the problem. "You have twelve thousand photos of your dog on here, Harry. How did you take so many so fast?"

He shrugged. "Bandit likes having his picture taken."

"Well, it's eating up all your memory." Riley

sighed and handed the phone back to him. "I suggest backing up to the cloud then deleting them off your device to free up more space. Storing them all on your phone is the problem. If you need help doing the backup, call the guys at the phone store."

"Okay," Harry grumbled while Riley led him to the elevators, biting back a smile. Despite all their quirks and her salty reputation these days, she loved the people in her town and didn't mind taking care of them when she could. She pushed the elevator button, and the doors whooshed open to reveal Sam standing there.

Her breath caught, same as it had when she'd come up behind him in line at the festival. He still looked just as dreamy today, though she herself felt frazzled and frumpy after a busy morning. She smoothed a hand over her hair to make sure it wasn't sticking up too badly.

Normally she didn't care much about how she looked, but she'd been hyperaware of it all since that night at the festival, when she'd realized her attraction to him might have become something more. She noticed everything about him now. Like the tiny gold flecks in his dark brown irises, and the white evenness of his teeth when he smiled at Harry, or how his scrub pants clung to his muscular thighs and butt just so...

She didn't realize she'd been ogling until Mr. Langston cleared his throat.

Whoops.

"Excuse me, youngsters." Harry sidled past them to get into the elevator. "Need to get downstairs."

Flustered, she moved her chair to the side, only to bump into Sam's leg. "Sorry."

"My fault," Sam countered, stepping back fast as if she'd burned him.

Harry harrumphed and shook his head as the elevator doors closed. "Saints preserve me from love."

Well, that was awkward.

Riley turned to head back to Radiology and her next patient, cursing herself for not remembering that this one had been referred by Sam for recurring migraines. Normally she kept on top of her referrals, but time had gotten away from her. As Sam followed her to the MRI suite, she asked, "How are you?"

"Good. Can't remember the last time someone called me a youngster." He seemed affable today. Always mercurial, that was her Sam. Sometimes the man seemed like a mystery wrapped in an enigma to Riley. He took a seat in the other chair at the desk beside hers in the reading room and nodded toward the observation window. "We can get started whenever you're ready."

Right. Turning her attention toward the patient where it belonged, Riley reviewed the woman's file to ensure she was doing the correct testing.

This was an MRI series of the brain to check for any vascular or structural changes or lesions that might be causing the patient's headaches. She signaled to the tech through the observation window to get the patient positioned correctly inside the machine. While that happened, she tried to make small talk with Sam to keep him from noticing how oddly she was acting around him today. Like leaning toward him without meaning to, as if drawn by an invisible connection. So strange. Whenever she caught herself, she leaned away again, embarrassed. She really needed to get control over this. "Did Ivy have fun at the festival?"

"It's all she's talked about for days," he said. "Now she wants skating lessons too."

"It's not a bad idea," Riley said. "I took them when I was little. It's good exercise, and that's one less gift to worry about for Christmas, right?"

"True." Sam looked over at her then, his dark eyes softening a bit. "It was fun having you and Adi there with us. I'm glad the girls found each other. It's helped bring Ivy out of her shell here."

Riley's chest pinched at this sweetness, and she kept her gaze on the file before her instead of the man beside her for fear he'd see what she was feeling in her eyes. "It's helped Adi too. After she lost her mom, we were all worried. She didn't talk for months, just beeped at people, imitating her favorite droid toy back then. Brock even took her to a speech therapist because of it, but they said it was trauma related and would go away on its own in time."

"Huh," Sam said, looking genuinely concerned. "Poor kid. Obviously they were right since she seems to talk fine now."

"Yeah. Some things just take time and patience." Riley shrugged. "Having Cassie return to town helped too. I think Adi just missed having a constant female presence in her life. She missed having a mom."

Sam seemed to take that in a moment, his lips pursed. He did that a lot when he thought deeply about things, she'd noticed. She really needed to stop noticing stuff about him. It was becoming a problem.

Finally, the tech signaled the patient was ready, and they began the MRI. It took about an hour overall, and the patient had been given IV gadolinium, a contrast solution to make the blood vessels in her brain more visible. When it was over, Riley and Sam went over the results together while the tech helped the patient out of the machine and removed the IV.

"On the positive side, there are no microbleeds, lesions or changes to the white or gray matter volume," Riley said, studying the images on her computer screen.

"True," Sam agreed over her shoulder, his body heat chasing away Riley's chill. "But on the negative, I still have no clue what's causing my patient's migraines." He sighed and sat back, rubbing his eyes, looking about as tired as Riley felt.

"You look like you need sleep," Riley told him, her stomach gurgling from hunger. "When's your shift over?"

"An hour ago," Sam replied, his tone gruff with fatigue. "But my replacement hadn't arrived yet at last check and this lady needed help, so I stayed."

"Are they here now?"

He checked his phone then smiled, looking rumpled and ridiculously sexy. Riley looked away fast, her face heating from her naughty thoughts. "Yes, thank goodness. Now I get to go home to an empty house and eat leftovers alone."

He didn't sound too disappointed, but Riley had been around him enough by now to hear the note of loneliness underlying his tone. It tugged at her heart and before she could stop herself, she said, "Or you could come home with me and eat leftovers there. Brock and Cassie are both working, and Adi and her baby brother are staying at her nanny's place tonight since we were all working."

Sam looked a bit startled, and Riley realized she shouldn't have suggested that because of their agreement. And sure, they might have crossed the line a bit the other night by sitting together at the festival, but that was a different situation. Neither had planned for that to happen. It'd been pure fate. This was a direct violation. The hint of the forbidden in her suggestion had her long-buried bad girl sitting up at attention. She played it down in her mind. This wasn't a big deal. It was two colleagues sharing a meal. They'd chat about work and cases and eat, then call it a night. End of story. Never mind that Riley seemed to be waking up from fevered dreams of her and Sam—in bed together, doing all sorts of wicked and wonderful things to each other—a lot lately.

"Oh, uh…" Sam shifted in his seat, fiddling with some papers on her desk. "I don't want to impose."

He was giving her an out. She should take it. Except she didn't. "You're not imposing. I invited you. Unless you'd rather sit in your house alone."

The silence stretched taut until the uncomfortableness grew too great, and Riley faced her computer again, the weight of Sam's stare still on her making the back of her neck tingle.

Finally, he exhaled slowly, as if surrendering at last to the inevitable. "Okay."

Riley swallowed hard then looked back at him over her shoulder. "Okay. Meet me at Brock's after you're done. My shift is done now too."

Sam nodded then left to go back downstairs to brief his replacement on the migraine patient's case. Riley finished up some last-minute documentation before clearing out and heading home.

Outside in the parking lot, she took a deep

breath of crisp winter air before clicking the buttons to remotely start her engine and open her vehicle. It had started snowing again, and after getting inside and turning on the heat, she checked her email on her phone while waiting for the windows to defrost. Lynette had messaged her again about the house on the bay. There were apparently other people scheduled to see the house tomorrow, and she wondered if Riley had found a contractor to give her estimates on the upgrades so she could put in an offer. The short answer was no. Riley hadn't contacted anyone because she'd been too busy. But she needed to do so fast if she didn't want this opportunity to pass her by.

Too many had done so already.

Once the windows thawed, Riley put her phone away and found a favorite rendition of "Have Yourself a Merry Little Christmas" by James Taylor on the radio before pulling out of the employee lot and heading toward home.

Once there, she let Winnie out in the fenced backyard to potty then heated up the leftovers from last night's dinner. By the time Sam arrived, everything was in the oven, and she'd changed into comfy jeans, socks, and a red sweatshirt with a reindeer and a large candy cane on the front that said "Pole Dancer."

Sam knocked at the front door and Winnie immediately lost her mind, paws scrabbling on the hardwood floors as she tore around the house in endless laps that would hopefully burn off all her excess energy before Riley went to bed.

"Smells good in here," Sam said as he took off his coat and hung it on a hook near the door before toeing off his snowy boots. "Anything I can help with?"

"The homemade mostaccioli and breadsticks should be done shortly, but you can set out plates and silverware, if you want." She led him into the kitchen and pointed out where things were kept. "We can eat in here at the island where it's cozier, or the dining room where we'd have more room. Your choice."

"The island works fine for me," he said, his grateful smile sending a fresh sizzle of forbidden attraction through her. "Thanks again for inviting me. I don't mind eating alone when I get home late, but it does get old after a while."

"You're welcome." To distract herself from the way her ovaries were jumping for joy because of his nearness, she asked, "You mentioned leftovers at your house. Does your nanny cook too?"

"No, I do. It relaxes me. Between the Italian dishes I learned from my wife and the Korean recipes I inherited from my mom, I can hold my own in the kitchen."

"Huh." Riley smiled, imagining Sam as a chef. "I was never much of a cook myself. Figured after the accident I wouldn't have to worry about it anymore because I wouldn't be able to reach stuff anyway. But then Brock had the contractors put in these adjustable-height countertops and other accessible amenities and now I don't have any excuses."

Sam chuckled, looking around. "Well, this kitchen is amazing."

"Yeah, it's going to be difficult to replicate when I get my own place."

"Maybe not." He shrugged. "Depending on what's in place to start with, the renovations could be more minimal than you think. I did all the work on our house back in San Diego myself to make it easier for Natalia once her condition declined. Kitchen, bathrooms, front entrance. All of it."

The oven timer dinged, and Riley grabbed a set of oven mitts from the counter to pull out the dishes of food, then set them on trivets on the island, using the time to gather her thoughts. She'd had no idea that Sam had handyman skills as well. Given all the other things he had going on that took up his time, she was intrigued. There were so many sides to him she'd yet to discover. She pulled out serving utensils from one of the drawers, then parked her chair beside his at the island to eat.

"Well, I looked at a house the other day that I really liked, but it needs a lot done to make it work for me," Riley said as she dished out mostaccioli for herself, then took a breadstick too.

"But I need to find a contractor to look at it with me to give me estimates so I can put an offer in if it fits within my budget. She said tonight that other people are interested in the property too, but I haven't had time to find anyone yet."

Sam swallowed a bite of his pasta then said, "I can take a look at it, if you want."

Riley frowned over at him. "Really? Are you sure? Your schedule is crazier than mine."

He scoffed. "Shouldn't take long. And I enjoy doing it. I learned young to fix things around the house to save money and honed my skills over the years. I'm not licensed here yet, but plan to be soon, before I'd touch your project. I understand though if you'd rather find someone else, what with our agreement and all—"

"No, no," Riley said. "That would be great. I know you, so I'd trust your opinions, and from what you've just told me, you'll know what needs to be done."

"Okay then."

"Okay."

Sam grinned as he bit off a bite of breadstick, and any awkwardness between them disappeared, just like that. "You'd be doing me a favor too, honestly. I like working with my hands but haven't had a chance to do much with my building skills since moving here. Renovating things gives me a sense of accomplishment too. A job well done. Kind of like surgery, except the house is my patient."

"That's very Zen of you," Riley teased, relief washing over her. For so long now she'd wanted to get a place of her own, but it had never seemed like the right moment. Something else always seemed to take precedence and it became so easy to put it on the back burner and forget about the dream. But now, with Sam basically offering her everything she needed, it was all right there waiting. She resisted the urge to hug him and instead picked up her phone. "I'll message Lynette now and see when she can get us in again."

After dinner, Sam couldn't quite believe he'd volunteered to help Riley with her renovations. But even worse, he couldn't bring himself to regret it. After the festival the other night, she seemed to occupy most of his waking thoughts, so why not go all out and keep hanging around her, even it went directly against their agreement? Neither of them seemed too upset about that, and it made him question where she was at with all this.

She'd offered to give him a tour of the rest of the house so he could get an idea of the kinds of things she'd want him to look at in the new place. Now they were standing in the hallway outside her bedroom, and he couldn't stop imagining if the circumstances were different and they were living together, even if it would never happen. He felt hot and bothered and wished he could quietly slip away, but with Riley's wheelchair blocking his escape route, that was all but impossible.

So, he forced himself to focus on the details of the architecture, the wide entrance to the room with its pocket door that opened and closed with the push of a button, the wide windows across the room with glorious views of Buzzards Bay, and the huge closet with automatic height-adjustable racks.

Next, they went down a ramp to the house's lower level, where a gym had been installed, again easily accessible for wheelchair users. In one corner was a hot tub, and at the sight of it, Sam's traitorous brain immediately clogged with images of Riley, slick and wearing nothing but a towel, before he banished those thoughts fast. He didn't want to think about her like that. He didn't want to want her that way. He didn't want to open his heart only to be left behind again. And yet it seemed that was exactly what was happening.

His chest constricted and beads of sweat broke out on his forehead.

"I realize it's a lot," Riley said, breaking him out of his anxiety spiral over the realization that despite all his efforts to the contrary, she'd found a way inside him, a way to make him open and vulnerable again. She made him want to throw caution to the wind and lose control with her. And that was…scary and stupid and sinfully appealing. She continued as his pulse jackhammered in his ears. "I don't really need any of this though. Just the basics upstairs would be fine to start." Then her gaze flickered down to his hands hanging by his sides, and her blue gaze flared with surprise. "You're trembling. Are you all right?"

Her eyes met his, concern and something he didn't know how to interpret logically within them. His body, however, had no problem grasping what was going on as a sudden, fierce need burned through him, a hunger for her that stole his breath, with her bright blue eyes and her lush dark hair and her quick intelligence. He'd tried to explain it away as nothing but loneliness. Tried to ignore it, deny it. But he knew now he couldn't continue like that. He wasn't ready, but then he might never *be* ready again. Riley had proven herself to be loyal and true and courageous. He needed to find those same traits in himself and stop using his grief and fear of being hurt as excuses to keep people at bay.

People like Riley.

She continued watching him, and he found the tilt of her head far more endearing than he should. She'd mentioned Adi missing a mother figure in her life. Ivy needed a mother too, deserved more than he could give her. But that was a lot for anyone to take on, especially someone who prized their independence as Riley clearly did. He didn't dare ask her. Not yet. Maybe not ever.

"We can take the elevator upstairs," she said, after what seemed like a small eternity, leading him over to a gold-toned door set into the wall. "This is something else you don't have to worry about since the house I'm looking at is all one level."

"Oh, uh, great." Sam tried to cover his discomfiture as the elevator door opened. They'd had an elevator installed in their old house back in San Diego too, but this one was much smaller. In fact, if Riley stretched out both arms from her chair, he bet she could touch both sides. Fitting them both in there together would be a snug fit. He hesitated, thinking maybe he could claim a phobia, but no—they'd already ridden in elevators together at work, so that was off the table.

So, they both boarded, and Riley pushed the button, which was at the perfect height for her in the chair. When the door closed, it was a tight enough fit to make his internal temperature tick up a notch. Thankfully, Riley kept talking, giving him something else to concentrate on besides her nearness and how easy it would be for him to pick her up and kiss her silly until neither of them cared about that stupid agreement they'd made.

"Like I said, my biggest concerns are the things I use every day. The counters, sinks, showers, windows, closets. Those will be the most important to have fixed by the time I move in."

"Sure," Sam said gruffly as the elevator whisked

them back up to the first floor. "It's just a matter of time and money."

"Everything's a matter of time and money." Riley snorted.

"Not everything," Sam countered, meeting her gaze, and now his skin felt too tight for his body.

"No, I suppose you're right," she said, her cheeks flushed as the elevator finally stopped and the door opened again, letting in a rush of blessedly cool air. "Not everything."

Sam held the door for Riley to exit first, then stepped out in the hallway after her. With the tour over and the air still sizzling with possibilities, Sam cleared his newly constricted throat. "I should be going. But thank you for dinner. And the tour. Let me know when the Realtor can fit us in."

"You're welcome. And I will." Riley smiled, looking around. She seemed happier tonight, more relaxed and open with him. He was enchanted. "It'll be hard to leave this place. I love it here. Even if my brother gets on my last nerve sometimes."

Sam pulled on his coat and shoved his feet into his boots, eager to get out into the frigid night to keep the fire inside him he now felt whenever Riley was around from scorching him alive. He pulled on his gloves and had a hand on the door handle, saying, "I'll talk to you soon."

"Okay. Be careful driving home," Riley said

from behind him, forcing him to turn slightly to avoid hitting her with the door, and that's when he saw she'd left her chair behind in the hall in favor of a pair of forearm crutches. She chuckled at whatever she saw on his face. Probably shock. In the whole time he'd known her, he'd only ever seen her in the chair. As if reading his mind, she said, "I've done a lot of PT over the last year. I hope to get back to walking on my own someday without these."

When she reached out to take the door from him, she bobbed slightly, and Sam automatically steadied her with a hand on her arm, but she pulled away fast. "I'm fine. I don't need help."

Sam froze, embarrassed heat creeping up his neck. Of course she didn't need his help. She was perfectly capable of handling things herself, just as his wife had been. Sam clenched his hands at his sides. "Sorry. I shouldn't have… Sorry."

"Stop apologizing. Please." She sighed, her shoulders slumping. "I'm sorry too. I know people say I'm salty about my situation." She made a vague gesture over herself. "But after my accident, Brock treated me like I was made of glass and would shatter at the slightest touch. It took me forever to get him to back off, so I could figure out how to survive on my own again. And once I move out, I won't have anyone around to open doors for me or pick up a crutch if I drop one, right?" Before he could say anything though, her phone buzzed, and she pulled it out of her pocket, balancing on one crutch. "It's a text from my Realtor. She has an opening tomorrow afternoon. Would that work for you?"

"What time?" He fumbled out his own phone, his palms slick with sweat despite the chilly air swirling around them both from the outside.

"Around two?"

"I'm free," he said, typing the appointment into his schedule.

"Excellent." She texted back her agent then gave him a cheeky grin. "Thanks again for helping me with this. It's an immense help. Especially so close to the holidays. This time of year can be so hectic."

"True. But I like to stay busy," he answered. "It helps keep the ghosts away."

Silence settled between them then, and when Riley finally spoke, her voice was lower than before, a bit rougher too, pulling on his heartstrings. "I still miss my parents, especially knowing it's my fault they aren't here. If I hadn't gone out that night, if I'd just listened to them about the guy I was dating then, that he was bad news…"

It was the second time she'd blamed herself for their deaths and he felt compelled to say, "That accident wasn't your fault."

"How would you know? You weren't here. They went out that night to pick me up after my date dumped me. During an ice storm. If that isn't my fault, I don't know what is." At the slight tremor in her voice, Sam clenched his fists to keep from pulling her into his arms and kissing her pain away. "I've learned to live with it."

"You shouldn't have to though." His tone held all the conviction welling up inside him. "You're right. I wasn't there. I don't know all the details. But I do know without a doubt that you were not responsible for what happened to them, Riley. We all make choices, and we live with the consequences. They could have sent a cab for you. They could have told you to ride home with someone else. They didn't have to drive there themselves. They chose to do that, Riley. And I can't imagine they would regret their decision. I know I wouldn't if I was in their place, rescuing Ivy."

She blinked at him, tears shining in her blue eyes, her mouth open like she wanted to say something to him. She reached out with her free hand, as if to touch him, and he leaned in toward her and...

The back door opened, and Adi ran inside, jarring them both back to reality. "Aunt Riley, why are you holding the front door open? I get in trouble when I do that."

Riley took a deep breath, as if trying to regain a little equilibrium. "Dr. Perkins was just leaving. And what are you doing home? I thought you were staying at Lois's tonight."

Brock came inside then too, closing the back

door behind him. "For once the ER was slow and overstaffed, so I volunteered to go home. Hey, Sam."

"Hey." Sam raised his hand in greeting, feeling far too exposed for his liking.

"Guess what!" Adi continued, rushing over to them. "Ivy and I are the *head* goldfish. Which means we get to swim in front of everyone on-stage and wave our fins at the audience!"

"Cool," Riley said as she closed the door again.

Sam crouched to put himself at eye level with the little girl. "I'm sure Ivy is excited too. She and Hala have been working on her costume. But being head goldfish means you both need to practice even more since you'll be in the spotlight. The play is only a week away now."

"The teacher said we don't have lines, so it's easier. She said we get to impoverish."

Riley looked at Sam, biting back a laugh. "I think you mean improvise."

"That's what I said," Adi said. "Improdise."

Sam chuckled and straightened. "Close enough. Who knew there were goldfish at the nativity?"

Adi ran back into the kitchen, where Brock stood in front of the fridge. "Daddy, can I have a Go-Gurt?"

"And on that note, I really am leaving this time," Sam said. "See you later."

"See you," Riley said, holding the door for him again as he hurried outside, grateful he hadn't embarrassed himself any more than he already had by kissing her again. If her brother had walked in and seen them… Talk about the rumor mill churning at the hospital.

And yet, as he got into his vehicle and began to pull away, he spotted Riley still in the doorway, watching him, looking as beautiful and bright as the Christmas Star, and thought that maybe people thinking he and Riley were a couple wouldn't be so horrible after all.

CHAPTER TEN

THEY SAW THE HOUSE the next day, which was how Sam ended up standing on the back patio, staring at the frozen splendor of Buzzards Bay. It was a good-sized outdoor space with Adirondack chairs and a small table that was included with the house. There was a small shed on one side as well, which he'd checked and found filled with hardware staples one might need around the house—lawn mower, Weedwacker, various tools, nails, screws, extension cords and a long length of rope. There were even a couple of inflatable toys for swimming in the summer. As he closed it back up, he realized how much he'd missed living near the water. There was a yearning inside him, growing stronger by the second, to spend more time here, to watch as the dark gray water lightened and changed as spring approached, to teach Ivy about the different animals that lived near the shore, to jog along the beach at sunrise. To walk hand in hand with Riley on the boardwalk as she used her crutches, stopping to kiss her near the water, hold her close and...

The thought froze him in place. He wasn't sure where that had come from, nor why, now that the thought was in his head, he couldn't seem to get it out. It should scare him witless to even consider being with someone like that again, in an intimate relationship. It would mean letting her into his life, his heart, his future. It would leave him exposed, vulnerable, quite possibly weaker and less in control. All things he'd steadfastly not wanted just a month ago, but now...

"So, what do you think?" Riley asked, joining him on the patio. "Can everything be done within my budget?"

"Based on my preliminary assessments, I think so," Sam said, glad to discuss something other than the uncomfortable emotions roiling inside him—deep affection, need, want, terror. He'd thought that by getting to know her better, his interest in her might fade. But it seemed the opposite was true. The more time he spent with Riley, the more time he wanted with her. She was brilliant in her career, passionate about those she cared for, and had obvious and genuine love for her family and community. She showered everyone in her circle with warmth and humor and concern—him and Ivy now included. If he'd been a man given to flights of fancy and fate, he'd almost believe their paths had been destined to cross.

When he realized she was still waiting for him to continue, Sam cleared his throat and added, "I'll still need to confirm supply costs with nearby retailers first, but you should be well within budget."

"Good!" Riley clapped with excitement. "I'll go tell Lynette I'm buying a house!"

Sam watched her go back inside, knowing the house was perfect for her: bright and open, the creative design somehow managing to perfectly merge the nature outside with the warm, cozy interior. There were even extra guest rooms so the girls could each have their own when they came to stay with her. Or if Riley decided to start a relationship and have children of her own at some point.

Except the thought of her being with anyone but him made him feel a streak of possessiveness that nearly made his knees buckle. Where had *that* come from? Riley didn't belong to him, and he didn't belong to her.

But you wish she did...

Perplexed, Sam shook off the strange thought. He didn't want a relationship. He didn't want romance. He didn't want to risk getting his heart eviscerated again.

Do I?

Just a month ago, he would've steadfastly said no. Now? He wasn't so sure.

Things had changed between him and Riley

recently, and while he was still processing it all, he also knew that those changes hadn't been all bad. He felt more connected now—to the town and to her. Felt a part of things again in a way he hadn't since Natalia was alive. Those were things he'd missed as well. Things he'd thought had been gone from his life forever.

Until now.

Deep in thought, he went back inside to join the discussion between Riley and her Realtor about the amount of the offer given the renovations that would need to be done. Once they'd hammered it all out, based on Sam's preliminary estimates for the work, the Realtor called the owners and made the offer, which they verbally accepted on the spot.

Riley was thrilled. Sam was too, on her behalf.

"Congratulations," Lynette said. "I'll get the paperwork ready, and we'll move forward."

"Any kind of time frame for closing?" Riley asked.

"I'd say after the first of the year sometime, considering Christmas is just two weeks away now." They left by the front door this time and the Realtor stopped at her car, parked near the curb, and turned back to them. "Happy holidays, you two. You make such a cute couple!"

Sam just blinked at the woman, too stunned to respond.

Riley didn't say anything either, at least until

her friend had pulled away. Then she turned to Sam and shook her head. "No idea why she thinks we're together."

"Hmm," he said, following her back into the house. It was a little warmer today, with a slight southerly breeze. The air stirred the hair around Riley's face, making Sam's fingertips itch with the urge to trace his fingers over her cheek, to see if her skin felt as soft as he remembered. Her sweet cinnamon scent teased his nose, and her warmth beckoned him closer. But it wasn't just sexual attraction anymore, Sam realized, though that was still as strong as ever.

A horn honked in the distance, snapping Sam back to reality, and he realized he and Riley had been watching each other this whole time, the moment stretching between them as heat raced through his chilled body.

Before he could second-guess himself, Sam leaned down and kissed her again. She made a soft, sexy sound and Sam couldn't get enough. He wrapped his arms around her, picking her up from her wheelchair and holding her to him, tangling his mouth with hers as the magic from their first kiss returned full force. Her breath mingled with his, her lips soft and warm beneath his own. If they hadn't been standing outside, in full view of everyone on the main street through town, he might have kept going. As it was, he pulled away slowly, feeling like the kiss had gone on an eternity, though it could only have been a few delicious seconds.

Had it been a mistake? Probably.

But Sam couldn't bring himself to care anymore.

He'd tried running, tried keeping everyone at bay all the time, tried avoiding Riley, tried denying his feelings, and it had been exhausting. Every time he saw her, their connection grew stronger, and the memories swarmed back, the feel of her mouth beneath his, her soft hair in his hands, her breasts brushing his chest as she clung to him. The scent and taste and feel of her... He couldn't resist anymore. He wanted to celebrate the rush of blood in his veins, the life-affirming surge of adrenaline that reminded Sam he was still very much alive and still very much a man.

Now he just needed to figure out how to move forward.

Riley was trying to figure out Sam Perkins while in her weekly PT appointment with Luna the next day. He'd kissed her twice now, and the way he looked at her sometimes was enough to scorch her panties, but he seemed to be holding himself back. Each time she thought they might take the next step forward, he seemed to move two steps back from her. It made no sense. She knew he was still dealing with his wife's passing, but this was ridiculous. Either he wanted her or he didn't. He needed to let her know.

"Earth to Riley," Luna said, giving her a flat look. They'd been doing passive range of motion exercises to help Riley warm up her hips, knees and ankle joints to keep them flexible and healthy. Over the last year or so, she'd worked hard to not only keep her leg muscles from atrophying, but to build new muscle mass too, all with the hopes of moving to the crutches permanently and leaving the wheelchair behind. "It's time to move to the bike."

"Sorry," Riley said, hiding her blush by wiping a towel over her sweaty face. "Distracted, I guess."

"Everything okay?" Luna asked, as Riley used her upper body strength to shift herself from the workout bench to a stationary recumbent bike beside her. It was designed especially for paraplegics, and the hospital had ordered it earlier in the year. In the quest to get Riley walking again, Luna said they had to address her circulation as part of the overall picture. Since then, Riley had utilized the bike as part of her weekly visits. Luna strapped Riley's right leg in the holder and her foot to the pedal then did the same on her left. Then she attached electrodes to Riley's right thigh and gluteus maximus muscles before stepping back. "Ready."

"Thanks." Riley flipped the switch on the control panel and chose the high-intensity mode, which involved four minutes of hard exercise with an equal interval of easier training to increase her blood flow and pulse, accelerating oxygen uptake and enhancing her heart's pumping volume. Once she'd really gotten going, Luna sat on the bench Riley had just vacated to keep an eye on her and make sure she wasn't overtaxing herself on the bike by keeping her talking.

"So, what's distracting you?" Luna asked again. "Please tell me it's something juicy and salacious. There hasn't been any good gossip around the place in months."

"I put an offer in on a house," Riley puffed. It wasn't a lie—she was thinking about that. But she was also thinking about Sam and their kiss yesterday. Not that she'd tell Luna about that. The last thing she wanted was the town talking about her and Sam, especially since they were still figuring out what was happening themselves. "Lynette said the closing should be after the first of the year."

"Wow. That's fantastic! Congratulations," Luna said. "Where's the new place located?"

Riley gave her all the details, still puffing slightly but not too winded. "It needs some renovations though." When she realized she'd talked herself into a corner, she tried to play it off as nonchalantly as possible. "Did you know Sam

Perkins also builds things? He offered to do the work for me."

"I did not know that." Luna sat forward. Why had she brought up Sam? Why? Too late now though, as her friend was giving her a Cheshire cat smile. "So, you and Sam have been spending a lot of time together, eh?"

"It's not like that." *Liar.* It was totally becoming like that. The heart rate monitor on the machine beeped at the sudden uptick of her pulse before Riley calmed herself. Stupid bike. She gave Luna an annoyed glance as she took a swig of water from the bottle attached to the bike, still peddling away. "He's helping me with the house. That's all."

"Sure." Luna grinned. "And he's your colleague."

"So?"

"And his daughter and Adi are friends."

"What are you getting at?" Riley snapped, beyond irritated now.

Luna shrugged. "Nothing. I think it's great that you two found each other. Lucille mentioned seeing you both at the festival and said you looked good together."

Riley stopped herself from telling Luna exactly where Lucille could shove her observations by scowling down at the digital screen in front of her as it tallied her progress on the imaginary course she was riding on. "We're just friends. And Lucille needs to mind her own business. After the way she outed Brock and Cassie on the town's Facebook page and dogged both you and Mark *and* Madi and Tate, I'd have thought you'd have stopped listening to her gossiping on principle."

"True." Luna shrugged then checked her watch. "Like I said, it's been slow around here. I'm sorry." She reached over and patted Riley's leg. "I really am happy for you, Riley. You deserve to find your someone too. Whether that's Sam or someone else, you need love."

"I don't need anything," she countered, wishing that were true. But since the day she and Sam started getting closer, she'd feared it wasn't. Not anymore. Despite all her determination to stay independent and prove she could do it all on her own, he'd somehow gotten past her barriers and made her see that maybe alone wasn't the best way to go. Riley pedaled harder, wishing she could ride away from her lingering fears about what commitment might mean for her but knowing she couldn't. "Sam's a good man."

"I'm sure he is." Luna sat forward, narrowing her blue eyes. "He seems extra good for you."

"I don't know what you're talking about." Even as she said it, Riley felt Luna's eye roll. "Okay, fine. We've kissed. A couple of times. But that's it."

"Kissing's good," Luna said, smiling.

"It was good," Riley conceded. "But now I'm not sure…" She struggled to find words to describe what was happening between her and Sam and how she felt about it all. "I don't know how he feels, and I'm scared that I'm going to lose the freedom I've worked so hard for, and it's all just messy and difficult, okay? So please don't say anything to anyone else about this right now."

"I promise." Luna leaned in, lowering her voice even though they were alone in the PT room. "Do you think Sam's The One?"

If Riley hadn't been strapped to the bike, she might've fallen off it she was so startled. Yes, Sam ticked a lot of the boxes of what she was looking for in a partner. He was smart and sweet and funny and thoughtful—and helpful to a fault. And he seemed to temper her more impulsive side well with his more logical approach to things. But she wasn't thinking too far into the future yet, not when her prognosis changed on what felt like a daily basis. She was taking things week by week at this point. "I do like him. A lot. But I'm not sure about more yet."

"Why not?" Luna frowned.

Because the future was complicated, with their pasts and their working relationship and his daughter. Neither one of them seemed ready to be in a relationship again, and Riley did not have the time or energy for pipe dreams. She'd worked too hard to get where she was now to surrender it all for a man who wasn't willing to let her have her freedom. And while she enjoyed being with

Sam, liked how he treated people with respect, no matter who they were, liked how he obviously wanted her too. But sometimes wanting wasn't enough. She couldn't afford to fall for him without knowing he'd be there to catch her.

Luna was still waiting for an answer, so Riley said, "I told you, it's complicated."

"Love always is," Luna said, giving her a sympathetic look. "You both need to talk. Stop running away from this just because you're scared. Trust me, I know how that goes."

"We're just being practical here. We lead very different lives."

"Different can be good."

"If both people are on the same page about it," Riley countered. "Sometimes I'm not sure Sam and I are even in the same book."

The bike finished its course and shut down, and Luna helped her undo the straps holding her legs to the machine before handing her the towel.

"Well, just don't give up too easily before you know what you've got, okay?" Luna said. "Trust me, the best things can happen when you least expect them. And the future you need isn't always the one you expected."

CHAPTER ELEVEN

THAT NIGHT, Sam was on edge as he drove through the lightly falling snow toward the Turner house. Not because of the weather, but because Ivy had come home from school that day and asked if she could spend the night at Adi's again so they could keep practicing for the Christmas play together. Sam wasn't sure how much practice being a goldfish took, but apparently it was a lot.

"Why are you mad, Daddy?" Ivy asked him from the passenger seat.

"I'm not mad, *yeobo*," Sam said, forcing his face to relax.

He was stressed after sitting through rounds of meetings at work all day. What they didn't tell you about when you accepted a department head position was the endless paperwork and bureaucracy that came with it. Yes, there was prestige and a nice bump in salary, but there were also days where the job was a real pain in the—

He inhaled deeply and rolled his tight shoulders, focusing on the road again until they pulled in under the portico in front of the Turner house a few minutes later. Ivy hurried out of the car while Sam shut off the engine, then he joined her at the front door. "I just want to make sure they know they don't have to pick you up from school tomorrow."

That, and he hoped to see Riley again, however briefly.

Yeah, he was a besotted fool.

"Okay," Ivy agreed, holding the old flip phone he'd given her last year in one hand and her overnight bag in the other.

Sam rang the bell then waited, his anticipation building until Riley answered the door, her hair piled atop her head in a messy bun. She was wearing a ruffled Christmas-patterned apron with streaks of flour across the front of her chest, which drew his attention there, reminding Sam of their kiss the day before. She was using her crutches tonight, and when she saw him, her face flushed, and her mouth opened as they both blinked at each other.

Riley found her voice first, which made sense since Sam wasn't sure he was capable of speech just then. "Hi, there. Come on in." To him, she whispered, "I didn't expect to see you tonight."

"Ivy!" Adi called, bounding into the living room where they were.

"I…uh…" Sam started, his words as jittery as his pulse. "I'm not staying. I uh…just wanted to let you know that I'll pick Ivy up from school to-morrow to take her to the hospital party. She'll text me when she's ready."

"Okay." Riley tilted her head adorably. "Cassie said it's no problem, though, if you have an emergency or something."

He nodded, noticing for the first time the smell of baking—something comforting and rich with sugar.

She gestured at her messy front. "We're making cookies for the hospital Christmas party to-morrow. You're welcome to stay and help if you want. It's just me and the girls tonight, since Madi and Tate are watching baby Ben, and Brock and Cassie are both working."

"Oh," he said, stepping back from the door. He hadn't planned on going to the party. Too many people. But he already wanted to spend more time with Riley, and he was pretty sure that urge would only worsen as the night went on. "I don't know…"

The girls ran over to join them. "Come on, Daddy," Ivy begged. "Please? It'll be so much fun!"

In the end, Sam couldn't resist the three faces looking back at him. He stepped inside and closed the door behind him, the tension inside him less-ening almost immediately. "Okay. I'm all yours."

Exclamations of glee erupted from the girls be-fore they raced down the hall to put Ivy's overnight bag in Adi's room, with Ivy telling Adi, "I brought my new skates with me. They're so cool!"

Riley smiled, shaking her head. "So, you got her the lessons, huh?"

"I did," he said as he took off his coat and boots. "You said it was a good idea and I believed you. They're the same skates as the ones she used at the festival, except white with glitter unicorns on the side. Ghastliest things I've ever seen, but she loves them." He shrugged. "She'll be going to the same rink as Adi too, but Ivy doesn't start until after the first of the year."

"You're a good dad," Riley said as she led him into the kitchen.

"I try." Her compliment made him feel ridiculously flattered, which was silly, but he didn't seem to be able to control his reactions around her anymore, and he was tired of trying. He stopped to pet the overly excited Frenchie dancing around his feet. "How's Winnie tonight?"

The dog gave a satisfied whine as he scratched behind her ears.

"I know," Sam said, grinning. "You and Spork need to meet."

"Who's Spork?"

"Our mutt."

"Ready to make cookies!" the girls shouted, their stockinged feet sliding on the hardwood floors as they ran back into the kitchen.

Sam noticed out the window that it was snowing harder now, the large flakes helping to set a very cozy scene. Growing up, they'd never had much money for gifts. And after Natalia's death, Christmas had become just another day to him. Tonight, though, he found himself excited for the upcoming holiday in a way he hadn't been in years.

They set up four frosting stations at the kitchen island, each person getting their own pan of cookies and frosting utensils, with bowls of different-colored frostings and sprinkles in the middle for everyone to share. As they worked their way through four dozen assorted stars, bells, reindeer and snowflakes, Sam was pretty sure more frosting ended up in their stomachs or on the girls' faces than on the cookies. Even Winnie got a dollop or five when some was dropped on the floor. Food coloring stained Sam's fingers, and the cuffs of his dress shirt, but he was so charmed by the whole affair he didn't even care.

After they finished, the girls got ready for bed while Sam and Riley handled the kitchen cleanup, working as a team to clear away the chaos. When they were done, Riley made them each a cup of peppermint tea, which they took into the living room to sip.

"That was fun," she said, taking a seat on the couch and setting her crutches to the side. "Thanks for helping."

"My pleasure," he said, meaning it. "I haven't done that in years."

"Making cookies was a tradition around here growing up. It felt right to revive it this year."

"Going to bed, Aunt Riley," Adi said, climbing up on Riley's lap to give her a kiss. "See you in the morning."

"Good night, munchkin," she said, kissing the top of her niece's head.

"Night, Daddy." Ivy clambered up beside Sam to hug him tight. "I love you."

"Love you too, *yeobo*," he said, hugging her tight before letting go. "Get some good sleep."

"We will," the girls said in unison before running off toward Adi's bedroom at the far end of the hall. The door closed with a resounding *thunk* behind them, cutting off their whispers and giggles. Sam bet they'd be lucky if they got a few hours of shut-eye that night, but they'd be fine.

Oh, to be that young again.

Once they were alone again, he and Riley sipped their tea as the snow continued outside, Sam's thoughts whirling like a blizzard in his head. He should talk to her, tell her how he was feeling. But what if she didn't feel the same? He felt like a gawky teenaged boy, which was probably why he ended up blurting, "About the kiss yesterday…" at the same time Riley said to him, "We should talk."

They both blinked at each other a moment before setting their cups aside and shifting slightly to face each other on the sofa.

"You first," Sam said.

"Okay." Riley took a deep breath. "I like you, Sam. A lot. Probably more than I should. But we made an agreement, which we've already violated several times. Based on the fact you've kissed me twice now, I think you like me too, but I can't read you. And I just need to know what we're doing here, because I don't want to get hurt again."

His brain had snagged on the *I like you, Sam. A lot* part, even though she'd kept talking.

"I don't want to get hurt again either." He needed her to understand, even though he wasn't sure he fully understood himself. "When my wife died, it nearly gutted me. We were partners, in every sense of the word. Losing her was like losing half of myself. I could barely function for months, just going through the motions of life on autopilot, and that's no way to live. I need to be fully present, for my patients, my daughter, my life. And the only way I could ensure that happening was by suppressing my emotions. I'd done a pretty good job of it too. Until I met you."

Riley watched him for a long moment, biting her lip. He'd never wanted to be a set of teeth more in his life. "What made you change?"

"You." Sam scrubbed a hand over his face. "You made me change. Don't ask me how or why, but I'm different now than I was even a month ago. I'm feeling everything again because of you, and I don't know how I can go back. I'm not sure I even want to."

She stared down at her hands in her lap, frowning. "That doesn't answer my question."

He sighed. "I like you too, Riley. So much it scares me."

Riley looked up then, their gazes locking as she swallowed hard, hesitancy and hope flaring in her blue eyes. "I'm scared too. I've tried to be independent for so long now, giving that up is hard."

"I don't want you to give that up," he said, his heart thumping in his chest. "I like you just as you are, Riley. Exactly as you are."

His urge to hold her and comfort her and kiss her broke through his self-control like an avalanche. Sam reached for Riley, pulling her to him and burying his face in her hair, unable to fight the pull of their connection any longer. "I don't know what we're doing either, but I know I don't want it to end."

Her gaze traveled over his face then, as she realized that he'd quickly become her favorite thing: his warm dark eyes, his firm lips, his golden-brown skin and his chin with the little divot in the middle. She traced her fingertips over each of his eyebrows, down the bridge of his nose, over his mouth. They'd have to be quiet. Very quiet.

And the knowledge it had to be secret made it hotter somehow.

Riley craved closeness with him, desire burning her from the inside out. Since the accident, she'd worried she'd never have this again, would never find someone who'd accept her completely, the good, the bad and the broken parts. Yet here was Sam, saying he wanted her just as she was. He saw her, really saw her, and that was a rare and precious thing. They might not have a clue how this would end, but there was no way she was turning her back on it now. Not tonight. Maybe not ever. "Let's go to my room."

Sam stood and swept her into his arms so fast, Riley gasped. She did love a bold man. As he carried her down the hall, she rested her hands on his shoulders, her nose buried at the base of his throat, inhaling his good Sam scent of pine and soap and crisp winter chill.

After locking the door, he let Riley slide slowly down his front until her toes barely touched the floor, his big hands at her waist, his warmth surrounding her, comforting her, driving her wild with lust. Fingers shaking slightly, she slid her palms down his biceps to rest on his forearms, their faces close.

Sam skimmed his lips over her left eyebrow, across her cheekbone, then settled his mouth into the notch just below her earlobe. Spirals of pleasure radiated out from Riley's center, like a prism of bright color shimmering over her skin as he nuzzled her neck.

"I want you so badly I ache," Sam whispered against her neck, lifting his head so his mouth rested against her ear as he pulled her closer still so she could feel the truth of it for herself. "I haven't been able to think about anything else since you came out of that dressing room in your tiny elf costume."

"Yeah?" Her voice came out husky as she arched against him. "And what are you going to do about it?"

"This." Sam kissed her slow and hot and deep, his legs bracketing her own, bracing her as his hands moved lower still, gripping her butt, rocking her into him, teasing the juncture between her thighs just right. Riley moaned and dug her hands into the front of his sweater, needing more, but not wanting to let him go.

Finally, both of them breathless with need, Sam picked Riley up and set her on the edge of the bed. They each tugged off their shirts and pants, leaving her in bra and panties and Sam in just jeans and socks. She licked her lips at the sight of his toned, lithe torso. She couldn't wait to explore every inch of him.

But he seemed to have other ideas first, opening Riley's legs to step between them, sliding his hands up her thighs so both of his thumbs pressed gently against her slick folds through her underwear. She stifled a muffled curse into his mouth and slid her fingers into his hair. Then he spread her thighs wider as one of his thumbs found her most sensitive nub through the lace of her underwear. He rubbed in slow, gentle circles, varying the pressure depending on how she gasped and moaned, finding what she liked best.

Riley groaned low as Sam bent over her, nipping her earlobe, his hot breath panting against her cheek. "You're so sexy."

Then he knelt before her, one hand holding her in place as he tugged off her panties with the other, exposing her to him completely. He swirled his tongue over her, then sucked gently, her grip in his hair tightening as her other hand scrabbled for purchase on the covers beneath her. Riley urged him on silently, arching into him, biting back her cries of pleasure, imagining what he'd feel like inside her.

Then Sam hummed against sensitive flesh and Riley went over the edge, her whole body vibrating as orgasm struck, washing her away on a tidal wave of endorphins and bliss until, finally, she came back to earth, chest heaving as she gazed up at Sam. He stood near the bed, watching her as he removed his jeans and boxer briefs. "Condom?"

"Nightstand."

He put one on then stretched out beside her, his erection brushing her hip. She was tired of waiting and wrapped her arms around him, pulling him atop her. Sam braced his weight on his elbows on either side of her head, his body pressed along hers as he settled between her legs, and she couldn't stop herself from reaching between them to stroke him. Riley took her time, running her loosely circled fingers up and down his shaft as he lavished attention on her breasts before finally settling into position between her legs again, his tip teasing her until she thought she might explode. "Hurry."

Sam laughed. "I like it when you're demanding."

In response, Riley pulled him down for another kiss as he entered her slowly.

"You feel amazing," he breathed, moving inside her. Riley lost herself to sensation, gripping his shoulders so tight her nails left little crescent-shaped marks, taking him deeper, holding him closer. She might not be able to feel her legs, but everything else was working just fine.

Sam buried his face in her neck, their soft moans swallowed in kisses and sighs.

"Yes. There. *Please*," Riley whispered as she changed angles, guiding him to what she liked best. Sam did not disappoint. He was watching her, his dark, fathomless eyes full of heat and yearning and desire. Before Riley knew it, she went over the edge again, climaxing hard, which sent Sam over the brink too. He went whipcord tight against her, his eyes closing until he collapsed atop her then rolled to her side, pulling her close, his heart racing against hers. Riley kissed his ear, too jelly-boned and satiated to do more. After a while, Riley expected him to leave, or pull away, but instead Sam burrowed closer. She laid her head on his shoulder and placed her hand on his chest.

"That was wonderful," he said, his tone sleepy. "But I think we need to go slowly. Is that okay?"

Riley exhaled with relief. "Yes. That's what I want too."

He got up then to use the bathroom, and Riley watched his retreating back, glad that he seemed happy, because that made her happy too.

And maybe, if they worked this right, they could both be happy, together.

Sam woke again a few hours later, taking far longer than he should have to realize he wasn't alone and this wasn't his bed. To be fair, he had a bit of a deep-sleep hangover. Between work and Riley and the approaching holidays, the last few days had been a blur of work emergencies. He sighed, remembering the last few hours. Making cookies. Making love.

Riley sighed in her sleep and curved her warm body more tightly against him, dealing him a death blow right in the feels. Being with her had been a revelation—sweet and shocking and shattering.

Sam took a deep breath and shifted to look over at her, finding Riley rolled up in the comforter like a burrito with only a puff of her shiny dark hair peeking out from beneath the covers. His heart squeezed with the urge to kiss her awake and repeat what they'd done earlier, maybe try a few new variations too.

Except...

He sat up and glanced at the clock on her night-stand. The girls would be up soon, and he needed to get out of here before that happened. To him, "taking it slow" meant keeping it a secret, at least for now. He needed to go home, take a shower and get to work so no one would know he'd slept here. With Riley.

Oh, God. What if Brock and Cassie were home? He hadn't heard anything, but that didn't mean anything. As tired as he'd been, a bear could've walked through the house and he might not have woken up.

Holding his breath, Sam inched toward the side of the bed, allowing himself a sigh of relief when Riley never so much as quivered. He hit the bath-room again, got dressed in his clothes from the night before, then snuck out of the bedroom to fumble for his boots and coat in the dark living room. So far, so good. The last thing he wanted was to explain to her brother what he was doing with Riley. Especially when he still wasn't com-pletely clear on it himself.

Was it a relationship? A fling? A "friends with benefits" situation? He had no clue. All he knew was that being with her had been glorious and he wasn't ready to share that with anyone else yet. Based on what Riley had said last night about not wanting to get hurt, or lose her freedom, he assumed they were on the same page there. Good.

Sam scratched his unshaven jaw. Flings and friends with benefits arrangements usually meant meaningless, no-strings, no-emotional-involvement kinds of sex. But that wasn't what he'd experienced last night with Riley. He took his boots over to the sofa to put them on in the dark, the moonlight streaming in through the windows highlighting the holiday decor, glitter and fairy lights and garlands galore.

Riley had mentioned while they'd frosted cookies that Adi had been given free rein with the design, and it showed. Sam had the same problem at his house because of Ivy. Apparently, according to seven-year-olds, decorating a house meant covering every visible surface to within an inch of its life.

Which turned his thoughts to Riley's new place. He pictured her living there, decorating for the holidays, trimming the tree and baking in her new kitchen. Maybe she'd have Ivy and Adi to help her. Maybe Sam would be invited again as well after he finished the renovations. Maybe…

For a second, he allowed himself to imagine

what it might be like to live with Riley, create a new life, a new future with her. The three of them sitting in the living room of the new house with Spork, watching the views of wintery Buzzards Bay through the windows, a tree glowing cheerily in the corner as they played games or read stories or streamed corny Hallmark movies on the TV.

It sounded wonderful.

With a sigh, Sam opened his eyes and returned to reality. He couldn't get carried away here. They still had a lot to contend with. Their pasts. Her need for independence. His need for control. Then there was the fact that his emotions were involved now—no point in denying it—and he was frightened. He felt confused and conflicted and completely out of control.

He had to be logical about this to protect them all. He stood to pull on his gloves and found Riley at the end of the hall, watching him from her wheelchair. She'd somehow snuck up on him without him knowing, still wrapped in the comforter and nothing else, her blue eyes shadowed and her dark hair tangled and sticking up all over her head. "I thought you'd left."

"I'm going now," he said quietly, bending to give her a quick kiss before heading for the door, ignoring the spike in his blood pressure from her nearness. He pulled his keys from his coat pocket, every fiber of his being telling him to go back to her, carry her back down the hall and get back into bed. "Don't want the girls to see me."

"See what?" Ivy's groggy voice came from the hall. She stumbled in, rubbing her eyes, her pj's crooked from sleep. "Why are you here, Daddy? Is it time to go home?"

Sam froze, his gaze darting from his daughter to Riley, then back again.

Fortunately, Riley moved faster than he did. "No, munchkin. Your dad forgot something last night, so he came to pick it up on his way into the hospital."

Ivy squinted through the dim light at him. "What'd you forget, Daddy?"

"Um…"

My sanity.

He searched for something, then held up his hands, wiggling his fingers. He hated lying to his daughter, but he could hardly tell her the truth.

"My gloves. It's cold and I needed them to keep my fingers warm."

Adi soon toddled in to join them, climbing into Riley's lap in the wheelchair. "Why is everybody up? It's time to sleep."

"I know, sweetie." Riley kissed her niece's head. "Sam just needed to get something first."

"And now I'm going." He opened the door, praying the slap of cold air on his face would wake him up from this nightmare. "Ivy, I'll see you after school."

With that, he rushed out of the house and over to his car, knowing this was a disaster. The girls talked to each other and the adults around them. All it would take was one word to the wrong person and the gossip machine in town would kick into overdrive. Everyone would know he and Riley were sleeping together. He started his engine to let it run while he cleaned off his windows.

Sam had to take control of this situation and prevent it from getting out of hand. Protect himself. Protect Riley. And most importantly, protect Ivy. He wasn't sure how to fix it yet, but he would. Because that's what he did.

CHAPTER TWELVE

"DON'T TELL ME you unwrapped your Secret Santa gift early and found Dr. Perkins inside, because if that's the case, there's gonna be a lot of single hospital workers who change what they put on their wish lists for next year," ER Nurse Madi Scott said as she stood beside Riley near the wall at the annual staff holiday party at Wyckford General.

Riley glanced across the crowded event room to where Sam stood, talking with several other doctors. She still wasn't sure how she felt about him leaving the way he had that morning, as if he'd been embarrassed or felt guilty about sleeping with her. Neither was a flattering reaction. Since then, they hadn't had a chance to talk, but each time their eyes locked across the room, her breath went a little haywire. Sam had been an amazing lover, seeming to know what Riley needed before she even knew it herself. Memories of the way he'd felt against her, inside her, filling her in a way that went beyond physical, in a way she hadn't experienced in years, kept floating through her mind at inopportune times. Like now. Riley felt wound tighter than a spool of Christmas ribbon.

Madi watched her closely, too closely, tapping the toe of her white sneaker against the floor, her coy smile letting Riley know that her friend wasn't buying her act where Sam was concerned. But there was no way she could know about them being together, regardless of what the girls might've said to other people. The gossip machine was good, but it wasn't that good.

"Seriously," Madi said. "I can tell something's bothering you. Might as well tell me now and save me the trouble of stuffing you with chocolate cake at the diner to get you to talk. Unless you want cake, in which case I'm always game for that."

"I'm fine," Riley said. And she was. She'd been fine before Sam had come into her life, and she'd be fine if he left. Even if it felt like a knife to the chest just thinking about it now. Besides, what would she tell Madi? That they'd had sex, but beyond that she had no clue what they were doing? Not exactly a stellar relationship report. If all this was even becoming a relationship, which, given Sam's reservations about all that, was unlikely at best…

"Sure you are," Madi said, not sounding convinced at all.

Riley took a deep breath. Her body was still tingling from last night, which was a nice change from the usual numbness. What they'd done the night before had been far more than sex for her. It had been a reawakening. The first time since her accident that she'd recaptured the old magic of intimacy she'd been missing so much. She'd had sex and orgasms over the past two years. She was human, after all. But it hadn't been as easy and carefree and wonderful as it had been with Sam. He'd seemed to enjoy their time together as much as she had, and while she didn't know every detail about Sam's life yet, she did know he wasn't a wham-bam-thank-you-ma'am sort of guy. He'd want to proceed with things. Of course he would.

She stifled the giddiness and uncertainty that had threatened to overwhelm her all day.

She was a strong, independent woman. She didn't need any man to make her happy or complete.

Now if her heart could just get with that program, she'd be all set.

Riley glanced his way again before she could stop herself, and just seeing him made her feel tangled up and twisted, which was enough to raise her anxiety levels to just short of panic. She wasn't in love with Sam. She wasn't. She didn't want to be in love.

"Does Brock know yet that you've found someone?" Madi asked.

"I have not found someone," Riley snapped. "Just because you and Tate are floating around on the Love Boat doesn't mean the rest of want to buy a ticket, okay?" She crossed her arms, feeling decidedly too exposed. Why couldn't people just mind their business? Hadn't they gotten a big enough piece of her after the accident, when everyone learned about what had happened?

Across the room, she watched Sam excuse himself and followed Lucille Munson through a doorway at the back of the room. Riley nibbled on cheese and crackers from the plate she'd made upon arriving at the party and cursed the itchy Santa hat on her head. Normally she liked these parties, but she wasn't in the mood for it now. The only reason she was staying was because Sam had been talked into playing Santa for the staff members' kids and Adi was going to be there, along with Ivy.

"Hey," Madi said after a moment, apparently taking Riley's silence for offense. "I'm sorry. I didn't mean to pry. I just really hope you find happiness again, Riley. You deserve it."

And now Riley felt bad. Madi was the nicest, sweetest person she knew. Riley knew her friend's concern came from a place of genuine caring. The same was true of Brock and most other people in town. But just because their concern was real didn't make it any less suffocating. If fact, what Riley wished for most right then was for everyone to stop worrying about her and what her future might look like and to just let her get on with it.

She found herself staring at the door Sam had disappeared through again, wondering if he had problems with his Santa suit. Maybe she should check on him...

"Psst... Dr. Turner?" someone called to Riley from the entrance nearby.

It was Daisy Randall. Riley excused herself then went over to talk to her. "How are you?"

"Good, thanks." Daisy looked better than she had during her last appointment. The PET scan results had come back unchanged, which was a good thing with ALS. It meant she had more time. How much? No one could say for certain, but then no one really knew how long anyone had left in life. Riley had learned that lesson the hard way. "My mom went to get the car. We were here to get lab work done and fill a prescription at the pharmacy. But I wanted to stop by and wish you happy holidays since I won't see you again before Christmas."

"Aw." Riley gave her a hug, their wheelchairs clacking together between them. "And happy holidays to you too. Do you and your family have plans?"

"Nah, we're sticking close to home for now. Enjoying the quiet."

"Sounds good. I'll be doing the same." Riley smiled. "Did I tell you I got a house?"

"How awesome!" Daisy beamed. "Tell me about it."

Riley did, including the fact that Sam would be helping her with renovations. Which reminded her—she needed to call Lynette about getting a set of keys so they could go in and take measurements. "I'm excited and can't wait for you to see it when it's done."

"Me too! And it'll give me incentive to live that long," Daisy added.

"Hey, new treatments are being discovered every day," Riley said. "Don't give up yet."

"Never." Daisy shrugged. "Just being realistic. But I swear I'll see your house, Doc. That's a new goal going on my vision board at home."

"Vision board? Maybe I should try one of those."

"Maybe. I'll let you get back to your party," Daisy said, peeking through the door. "Looks like fun."

"You want to come in?" Riley asked. "It's mainly staff and their kids, but Sam's playing Santa."

"Dr. Perkins? Really?" Daisy seemed as surprised as Riley had been at hearing the news. She checked her watch. "I wish I could, but Mom's waiting. I'll see you at my next appointment." She waved and turned away, then stopped and called back, "And happy New Year, Doc!"

Riley returned to her spot against the wall just as Adi and Ivy arrived. Her niece ran over and scrambled up onto her lap. "Aunt Riley, is Santa here yet?"

"Not yet, kiddo." Riley ruffled her hair. "But soon."

"Hey." Brock leaned against the wall next to her. He must've been pulling office hours in their dad's old clinic that day, because instead of scrubs he had on trousers and a shirt and tie beneath his lab coat. His stethoscope was still around his neck too, meaning he'd probably left in a hurry. "We miss anything?"

"Just mediocre snacks and warm eggnog." Riley shrugged as her niece raced over to where Ivy stood watching a man making balloon reindeer. Or at least that's what they called them. They looked more like dogs to Riley. "Where's Cassie?"

"Consulting on a facial reconstructive case," he said. "She probably won't make it."

"Lucky her."

"I see your holiday spirits are alive and well." He chuckled, resting his head back against the wall.

"My spirits are great," she grumbled, knowing she needed to tell him about buying the house.

Now seemed as good a time as any, so she said, "I need to tell you something."

Brock laughed outright now. "What? That you and Sam Perkins have a thing going?"

"What!" Riley turned to look at him so fast she almost gave herself whiplash. "Why would you say that?"

If the rumor mill got ahold of what they were doing, it would be awful. She didn't think she could take being the focus of all that attention again.

Her brother shrugged. "I have eyeballs, sis. You two have been giving each other puppy dog looks for weeks now."

"Have not!" She knew she sounded childish, but then so was this conversation. She didn't owe anyone an explanation for how she lived her life. "And why is it any of your business anyway?"

"Calm down, Salty Queen," Brock said just as the door opened across the room and Sam stepped out. Brock narrowed his eyes, then laughed. "Sam is Santa?"

"Yes." She tried to refocus the conversation on more important matters. "I need to tell you that I—"

He pushed away from the wall as Adi and Ivy raced toward where a line was forming to see the big guy in red. "Sorry. It'll have to wait. I need to keep my daughter from climbing your new boy-friend like a Christmas tree."

"He's not my boyfriend! We work together, that's all!" Riley yelled after him, too loudly given that everyone within range of her turned to look at her, including Sam. As usual, she couldn't read his reaction, especially when he had that big white beard on, but it didn't matter.

"I bought a house," she told Brock bluntly. She'd tried to ease into it but, given the situation, that wasn't working. "My closing is after the first of the year and I'll be moving out shortly thereafter."

Brock just blinked at her. "What?"

"I bought a house," she repeated, feeling a little bad about telling him like this, but there never seemed to be a good time and, well, she needed to get on with her life. Besides, it wasn't like she'd planned to stay with him forever anyway. "It's on the bay, not far from you, so I'll still be able to watch Adi if you need and we'll still see each other a lot. I just really need a place of my own now, for privacy, and that way you and Cassie have more room too."

"But things are going so well the way they are. I thought you were happy living with us." His expression was an odd mix of surprise and hurt. "Are you sure you're ready to be on your own?"

"I *am* happy at your place, and I'll always be grateful for you taking me in after the accident, but yes. I'm ready to be on my own." She squared her shoulders. "This is for the best."

"Is it?" Brock crossed his arms, narrowing his gaze. "Is the new house accessible? If not, how are you going to get around and do things by yourself? Have you thought of that?"

Affront quickly burned through her guilt over dropping a bombshell on him at the staff party. "I'm not an idiot. Of course I've thought of that. I've got it taken care of. A contractor is going to be renovating it for me before I move in. I'm using your house as my guide because you did such a good job. Quit worrying about me."

"I can't stop worrying about you," Brock growled. "You're my sister."

"Exactly. You're my brother, not my keeper or my boss. I'm moving out. Deal with it," she said, mirroring his obstinate posture. "Fighting about this is stupid. We're both grown adults. We can both do what we want. I can take care of myself. Always have, always will."

"Who's doing the work for you?" he asked, ever overprotective. "Are they licensed?"

"Which part of 'not an idiot' didn't you understand?" she asked, again probably too loudly, since people nearby were watching them now. She'd hoped Santa's arrival would give them cover, but apparently not. "Believe it or not, brother, you're not the only one who knows how to get things done." She thought about lying to him about who was doing the work for her but figured he'd find out soon enough anyway, so she came out with it. "And Sam's doing the work for me."

"Sam Perkins?" Brock's nose scrunched in disbelief. "What the hell does he know about renovations?"

"He renovated his own house back in California. He's been doing them for years. It's his hobby, he said. And he has experience with accessible homes. He's perfect for the job."

"Really?" Her brother did not sound convinced. "I don't believe it."

"I don't care what you believe." She'd known her moving out was going to be an issue. Brock had always been way too bossy for her taste, and with his previous golden boy stature in town, it had made him way too big for his britches. She'd thought the accident had tempered his attitude, but it obviously hadn't. Thirty-two years of resentment, coupled with the stress of not knowing what was happening between her and Sam, congealed into a flaming hot mess of anger. "Why can't you let me have this, Brock? For three decades I've lived in your shadow, never quite reaching the spotlight no matter how hard I tried. Now, finally, I get to have this one thing for myself, and you still can't be happy for me. All you want to do is control me and keep me under your thumb. Well, no more. I've had enough!"

"Daddy!" Adi yelled as she ran over to them.

"Santa said he'll bring me a seven-foot-tall Darth Vader for Christmas!"

Brock's blue eyes still blazed with fury as he glared at Riley, and she knew their discussion wasn't over—just paused. Fine. She was glad she'd put it all out there. It was past time. And if it was news to him, all the better. She'd kept it inside too long.

To his daughter, Brock said, "We'll talk about Santa later. Can you go get me a cup of eggnog?"

"Sure!" Adi said, skipping off, completely oblivious to the sizzling tension between her father and her aunt.

"First of all," Brock said, which was never a good conversation starter, "I don't know what the hell you're talking about. Living in my shadow? You were the baby of the family. You got all the attention and never even had to try. I had to practically bend over backward just to eke by."

"Whatever," she snapped. "Everyone in town loved you! The big hero!"

"Hero?" He gave her an incredulous look. "After Kaede died, I was a wreck. You know that. I couldn't even get out of bed for days. And when I did, it was just to make sure Adi was still okay. What kind of heroics is that?"

She opened her mouth to answer, but he talked right over her, which only annoyed her more. An ear-splitting scream ripped through the air from somewhere near the dais, where Sam was sitting with a kid on his lap, but the fight was going too strong now for either of them to pay much attention. They hadn't had a row like this in decades, and it was long overdue.

"You got away with everything growing up, Riley. Everything. Late nights, breaking curfew, running around with the wrong crowd. Anyone would look golden compared to that. And if I tried to do the opposite just to get a bit of attention, can you blame me? And after all I did for you after the accident too."

"I never asked you to do any of that," she countered. "I've told you over and over how grateful I am that you took me in, and I am. But I never asked you to do it."

"So I was just supposed to leave you to fend for yourself?"

"Yes! Maybe if you had, I'd be out of this chair already from necessity."

"Oh, do not put that on me. If you're going to blame anything for what happened to you, then—"

"What? Blame myself? I do, believe me. I know that accident was my fault, Brock. I don't need you to tell me that, okay? I think about the fact that our parents are dead because of me every single day!"

When Sam emerged from the back room, dressed as Santa, he asked himself for the umpteenth time how the hell he'd been talked into this. But he already knew why: because someone needed help and it was his duty to answer the call. So now here he was, at the front of the room on a dais, swathed in hot fabric and fake white fur stuck to his neck and chin, pretending to be jolly old St. Nick on short notice.

He glanced across the room and spotted Riley talking to Daisy Randall in the doorway. He'd tried to avoid looking at her as much as possible before changing for fear someone would see his feelings written all over his face. Last night had been a revelation for him. The way she'd responded to him, the sounds she'd made, the taste of her on his tongue… At first he'd thought sleeping with her might have broken the spell between them, but the opposite was true. The more he got of Riley, the more he craved. She made him believe in the magic of Christmas again. She made him feel better, less alone. She made him forget everything but her—including right now.

Lucille, dressed as a North Pole helper for the party, cleared her throat, letting him know the line was ready for him.

Right. Showtime.

He nudged the big bag of toys on the floor by his feet and gave a hearty *ho, ho, ho.* "Welcome, kids and kids at heart! Who's ready to come up and get a gift from Santa and to tell me what you want for Christmas?"

The children in line, including Ivy and Adi, jumped and clapped and whooped for joy. Santa was a legend to them and now Sam was representing him today. He swallowed hard and gestured for Lucille to send the first child up. The whole party was a bit much for him, but Wyckford General seemed to go all out for its staff and their families.

The first few children were easy enough, asking for the normal stuff—toys, sports equipment, tech gadgets. Then came Adi. She climbed up onto his lap, immediately called him Dr. Perkins, then asked for some giant *Star Wars* thing, and since Sam had no clue what it was, he said he'd do his best to bring it to her. He'd mention it to Brock later just in case.

Ivy went fine too. He'd made note of all the things she'd wanted and would do his best to get everything on the list, whether locally or online. He'd already purchased the train set she'd liked the day they'd played bingo, and just had to find time to pick it up from the store.

He saw a few more kids then, the line steadily decreasing in length as he kept the visits short and sweet. And while the holidays were not bittersweet for him, he still loved seeing the joy and wonder on children's faces this time of year and how people were nicer and more considerate to one another. And yes, Natalia's death had dulled his happiness for the past couple of years, but now he felt like a bit of his old spirit was back. And while he could kid himself all he wanted about the source of that new spark, the truth of it was that it was all because of Riley.

He glanced over to where she was talking to her brother against the far wall. They seemed deep in serious conversation, and her face was flushed, but before he could wonder if he should be concerned, the last kid in line was plunked down onto his lap by Lucille. It was a little boy who looked to be about three.

"Hello!" Sam said to him. "What's your name?"

After squirming a bit and poking a knee far too close to Sam's privates for his comfort, the boy blinked up at him, wide-eyed. "R-Ronnie."

"Well, Ronnie…" Sam adjusted the youngster on his lap to a more comfortable position. "Why don't you tell Santa what you want for Christmas?"

"No!" the little boy shouted, struggling now to get down, his face red and his expression belligerent. "I want my mommy!"

He glanced over to see one of the labor and delivery nurses dressed in pink scrubs standing near the sidelines, looking apologetic. Sam gave her a nod and a smile to let her know it was fine, then held on to Ronnie a bit tighter as the kid made a valiant effort to escape. His small legs swung wildly, and this time his heel caught Sam in the shin, sending a painful jolt up his right leg. He gasped and automatically reached for his leg, allowing Ronnie precious time to reach up and tug his beard off. Then the boy screamed—an ear-splitting, blood-curdling keen that only a terrified toddler could produce, followed by something warm and wet soaking through the leg of Sam's Santa suit. Pee. Wonderful.

"Oh, God." The poor mother ran up to collect her sobbing child. "I'm so sorry, Dr. Perkins. Ronnie's usually such a good boy. He was hungry and I should've taken him through the food line first, but I'm on my break and thought this would be faster."

"No, no," Sam assured her, wincing slightly as he tugged the wet material of his pants from his leg. He looked out into the room then, to see who had witnessed his humiliation, but found everyone watching Riley and Brock as they had a rapidly escalating argument. As the mother carried young Ronnie away, the room quieted enough for him to hear the yelling coming from across the room.

"I think about the fact that our parents are dead because of me every single day!"

Oh, boy.

Riley had told him as much the other night, and he'd assured her that the accident hadn't been her fault. He still believed that with every fiber of his being, but she obviously didn't. He stood to go back to the dressing room to clean up and change, when Adi ran back to her father with a cup of eggnog in her hand.

"Here, Daddy," she said excitedly into the quiet. "Aunt Riley, is Sam spending the night again to-night, since Ivy is?"

Sam felt the gasp that went through the crowd over every inch of his prickling skin. He froze, not sure what to do. His worst fear was being vulnerable, exposed, and now his deepest secret had been shared with a room full of people not known for being discreet when it came to gossip. His chest constricted and his mouth felt hollow as Riley's gaze met his across the space.

Time slowed again, but not in the romantic way it had before with them. This was more like a slow-mo disaster.

Brock glanced from Riley to Sam then back again, his tone turning decidedly accusatory. "What the hell is my daughter talking about? Are you sleeping with Sam Perkins? In my house?"

Riley opened her mouth, closed it, then opened it again, her cheeks deep pink now. "That's none of your business!"

People were whispering and glancing between Sam and Riley now, clearly enjoying the show, and all he wanted to do at that moment was hide. Burrow himself away somewhere safe and dark and protect himself and Ivy and Riley from what-ever wanted to harm them.

But he knew Riley wouldn't want that, and he

didn't know what else to do other than explain himself, so instead of changing, he stepped off the dais and headed across the room. "Brock, if you'll let me explain—"

"I don't want to hear it from you, Perkins. I want to hear it from my sister," Brock said, his gaze steady on Riley. "Are you and Sam sleeping together? Is that why you want to move out all of a sudden?"

She shot visual daggers at her brother. "I want to move out so I can get you out of my business! You have no right to question me or what I do." She grabbed her chair wheels and started to move toward the door. Except partway there, she got caught up in a tree skirt that had been knocked askew by the crowd. She struggled to get it out of the way, and without thinking, Sam rushed over to help her.

"Get away from me!" she all but snarled at him, unshed tears glistening in her blue eyes, nearly breaking Sam's heart. "I've got it myself. I don't need you and I don't need your help. Just leave me alone! For good!" She yanked hard at the tree skirt, and it ripped in two, freeing her chair wheel at last. She'd obviously had it with everyone by this point and just wanted to be alone. He should have known that, should have given her space, but it seemed he'd failed. Again. "And go change your clothes. You smell like pee!"

She rolled out of the room and toward the elevators, leaving him behind to stare after her, his wet, stinky pants sticking to his leg and his shattered heart in pieces on the floor.

"Daddy!" Ivy said, sniffling as she came up to him. "I want to go home now. Everyone's staring at us."

"I know, *yeobo*," he said, placing his hand atop her head. He'd known better than to open himself up again, because it only led to pain in the end, and now it wasn't just him who was the center of everyone's negative attention—it was Ivy too. His hurt nearly made him stumble, but he had to be strong for her. "Let me change, and then we'll go. Why don't you and Adi go and use the restroom before we leave?"

"Sam," Brock said as the girls left, and the room's attention shifted away from them at last. The man looked shell-shocked and more than a little chastised. Good. Whatever had started that fight, Brock should have been adult enough to not have had it here in front of everyone. Sam was angry too. Angry and hurt and left completely torn asunder. His first instinct was to go after Riley, but she needed time to cool off. They all did. Best to leave it alone, give it time, then sort through the aftermath. Though something in his gut told him it was over. It never should have started. He knew better than to trust his heart and his emotions. He couldn't protect Riley from hurt, that much was clear. Just like he hadn't been able to protect his wife. He just wasn't good enough...

And yet he'd gone and fallen for Riley anyway.

"Did you know those giant animated Darth Vader things cost upwards of a thousand dollars?" Brock was saying. "Not to mention they're almost impossible to find. Maybe you should think about that before you make a promise you can't deliver on."

He stalked off, leaving Sam alone. Great. He'd pretty much disappointed everyone now. As he walked back to the dressing room in his urine-soaked pants, he decided Brock was right. He should have thought about a lot of things before making promises he couldn't deliver on.

CHAPTER THIRTEEN

THE NEXT WEEK passed in an awkward blur of longing and regret for Riley where Sam was concerned. She regretted the way they'd left things at the party, and how she'd lashed out at him when he'd only been trying to help her, but she'd been hurt and embarrassed and all she'd wanted to do at that point was get away from everyone to calm down and collect herself. But she'd also expected him to come after her at some point. When he hadn't, she hadn't been sure how to interpret that.

They'd only had the one night together, after all, and while it had been spectacular, Riley also knew how skittish Sam was when it came to privacy and relationships. They'd blown both of those things out of the water at the party, in front of half the hospital staff. Since then, she'd not heard anyone directly discussing the big fight in front of her, but it was apparent people *were* talking about it, about her, by the way they stop talking whenever she was nearby.

So yeah, she and Sam had steered clear of each other since the party.

She wasn't actively avoiding him. She was still at work, still seeing her patients, and assumed he was seeing his to, but their paths hadn't crossed at all. Which was strange because, while they were both busy, the hospital wasn't that big, and they'd usually at least pass in the halls. So maybe he'd gone out of his way not to see her.

One person she *was* sure was avoiding her was Brock. Since the party, they hadn't said two words to each other, which for two people living under the same roof was hard to do. Their whole argument had escalated way too far, way too fast at the party, and she felt bad about it. But Riley also still stood behind the fact that what she'd told him had needed to be said. He'd seemed stunned by her words, but what surprised her more was his denial about her being in his shadow all this time. How he felt like he'd had to fight for attention because she'd taken all of it.

It was the farthest thing from the truth, but also oddly fascinating. In all these years, she'd never really looked at their situation growing up from his perspective. She supposed maybe she had gotten away with a little more, but that was because their parents had always been so focused on Brock's accomplishments.

Hadn't they?

Well, whatever. It was done. Over with. Both her fight with Brock and her fling with Sam.

And while it hadn't felt temporary to her, it was probably good it was over because they still had to work together, both at the hospital and on her new house. Which was where she was now, waiting for Sam to show up to take measurements. Riley had come earlier, bringing Adi with her, because yeah, she was nervous to see Sam alone again.

Would he be angry with her? Resigned to the end of their…whatever it was? Sad and stressed, like she was?

"Can I go out on the patio?" Adi asked her as they stood in the kitchen. She had her skates around her neck, the laces knotted together. Riley had picked her up at the rink after her last lesson before the holidays.

"Uh, sure," Riley said. "But stay away from the beach. It's too cold. It's icy but not fully frozen through yet. It's not safe to walk out on, okay? And keep your gloves on."

"Okay." The little girl went outside to play with her toys as a knock sounded on the front door.

Sam.

Riley's pulse jittered with nerves. She wasn't ready for this. She wished they could go back to before that stupid party and redo it all to not have that stupid fight, to not draw the attention of everyone in the room to them and all their secrets.

Another knock, and Riley took a deep breath before smoothing a hand down the front of her sweater. She'd used her crutches today since it had been a while since the last snowfall and the streets and sidewalks were clear now. She hobbled to the front foyer and said a silent prayer for strength as she opened the door to find Sam and Ivy on the stoop. He had a frown on his face and a toolbox in one hand. Ivy had her backpack.

"Come in," Riley said, flashing a nervous smile. "Adi's out back on the patio, Ivy, if you want to play with her."

"Cool! Thanks," Ivy said, skipping off to find her bestie.

It seemed she'd recovered well enough after the trauma of the other day. Riley only hoped she and Sam could do the same, but she had her doubts. He walked past her into the hallway, the breeze carrying his good Sam scent, and she found herself inhaling deep as she closed the door. She'd missed him, even if it had just been a few days.

"Where do you want me to start?" he asked when she returned to the kitchen. His voice sounded lower, gruffer, than it usually did, and she wondered if he was nervous too. He'd laid out different tools on the granite island—tape measure, pencils, a laser guide—and was shrugging out of his coat to reveal a dark green sweatshirt underneath. He looked comfortable and casual in his jeans and work boots. Handsome too. Riley fought the urge to throw her arms around him and hold on for dear life.

He wasn't hers to hold.

"Uh, wherever you think is best. You're the expert."

Sam snorted as if she'd made a joke, then picked up his tape measure and a pencil and headed for the master bedroom to check the closet and bathroom. Riley tagged along behind him, feeling as useless as tits on a bull. Given that she needed both hands for her crutches, she couldn't even hold the tape measure for him. Not that he asked. Generally, he seemed to give her an extra-wide berth, going out of his way to make sure they didn't touch at all, even in passing.

Guess that answered her question about what the future held for them.

Finally, when he'd checked all the closets and bathrooms and returned to do the kitchen last, Riley couldn't stand it anymore. She waited until he'd crouched in front of a set of lower cabinets then said, "I'm really sorry about what happened at the party."

He straightened, focusing on typing his measurements into his phone as if she hadn't spoken. She glanced through the sliding glass doors to where Ivy and Adi were playing on the back deck. Ivy was trying on Adi's skates.

"You have every right to be mad at me," she added.

"I'm not mad at you, Riley," he said finally. "I'm mad at myself."

Now it was her turn to frown. "Why? What did you do?"

Sam continued measuring the kitchen. "I failed to protect you. I made bad decisions where you're concerned, and now we're paying the price for that. I'm sorry."

Hackles rising, she gripped the edge of the island tight. "Bad decisions?"

"Yes. I thought I was ready to get involved again. I thought I could compartmentalize what was happening between us. Control it. Keep it from causing issues in other areas of my life. I couldn't. And because I couldn't, I caused you stress and upset and created a rift between you and your family."

It took her a moment to process all that, but when she had, her anger rose. "Wow. So, you're saying this is all your fault?"

"Yep." He crouched again to measure the dishwasher, and she did her best to ignore how good his butt looked in those jeans. She did not need to be looking at that right now.

"Wrong." She hobbled over closer to him so that when he stood once more, they were facing each other. "This was not all your fault. I did plenty on my own before you ever showed up in your Santa suit, buddy. And just so you know, that rift between me and Brock was a long time coming, okay? You don't get to control that narrative either, sir."

"I'm not trying to control anything, Riley. I'm just stating the facts as I see them."

"As you see them. But not necessarily as things are."

A muscle ticked near his tense jaw. "And how do you think things are?"

"I think we both took a chance on being together and it was always going to be rocky at first. I thought you were the kind of guy who wouldn't run at the first sign of turbulence. I thought you were the overprotective alpha type. Kind of like Brock. Apparently, I was wrong."

His lips tightened a bit at the direct hit on his vulnerabilities. "I'm not running. I'm being logical."

"Oh, really? Because from where I'm standing it looks an awful lot like avoidance."

For a second, it looked like Sam wanted to argue more about that, but then he turned to put his coat back on. "I have what I need here." He shoved his phone back into his pocket. "I'll get quotes on supplies and then—"

The rest of his words were drowned out by a scream from outside—a heart-ripping, life-in-danger sound that had both her and Sam running out onto the patio to find both girls gone.

"What the—" Sam took off down the board-walk leading from the patio to the beach with

Riley doing her best to keep up on her crutches. She prided herself on her independence and being able to do everything other people could, but sometimes being differently abled really sucked.

"Adi? Where's Ivy?" Sam shouted as they reached her niece. "What's happened?"

Adi was sobbing so hard all she could do was point out toward the bay, where a dark hole was visible in the frozen ice on the bay, maybe fifteen feet from shore. Riley knew the drop-off around there was sharp and deep, and her stomach sank to her toes. She remembered Ivy trying on Adi's skates.

"Did she go out on the ice?" Riley asked.

Adi nodded, her breathing jagged as her teeth chattered so hard her words stuttered. "I—I told her not to go. Not like the r-rink. The bay—the bay kills p-people. K-killed my mom, and now I-Ivy t-too!"

Sam swore under his breath and ran back up the boardwalk to the patio and headed straight for the shed, where he grabbed a coil of rope then ran back. He tossed Riley his phone before tying the rope around himself in a makeshift harness then handed her the other end. "Call 911. I'm going in to get my daughter."

"Wait!" Riley yelled after him. "Sam! You can't go out there. It's too dangerous!"

"I have to!" He stopped at the edge of the frozen bay and turned back to her. "If we wait until help arrives, it will be too late. I was on a volunteer rescue dive team back in San Diego. It's not quite the same circumstances, but I do have some training. I can't lose Ivy! She's all I have left."

Riley dialed 911 as Sam slowly made his way toward the hole in the ice. She reported their emergency, and the dispatcher told her fire rescue was five minutes out. Sam was right. That would be too late.

She's all I have left...

Her chest squeezed at his words, knowing that wasn't true. Not anymore. He had Riley too. If he still wanted her.

From the ice, Sam yelled back at her, "Wait for my signal to pull."

Sam dropped to his knees about five feet from the hole and crawled the rest of the way, the ice cracking ominously beneath his weight. Then, in the blink of an eye, it gave way and Sam dropped into the frigid depths. Riley choked back a scream as he braced his gloved hands on the edge of the new hole he'd just created, taking a deep breath before going under again to search for Ivy. Based on his body mass and the temperatures, Riley knew he had about thirty minutes before becoming hypothermic. Now they had two clocks running: one for Ivy and one for him. She prayed he'd save them both before time ran out.

Sam pulled himself out once more, then disappeared again beneath the surface. Riley counted the seconds, praying that Sam knew what he was doing, her hand tightening around the rope. Maybe all that upper body work she'd done with Luna in PT would finally pay off. Each time she closed her eyes, flashbacks of the accident slammed into her with debilitating force. Trapped and submerged in the freezing, unforgiving darkness as her injured parents drowned before her eyes, with Riley paralyzed and helpless in the back seat. She refused to be helpless ever again.

"Aunt Riley, it's them!" Adi yelled.

Her eyes opened wide to see Sam pop out of the water one last time, this time clutching his daughter's limp body. He finally gave Riley a thumbs-up and she dug her feet into the sand and tugged with all her might. Adi picked up the slack behind her and pulled too.

They hauled on the rope at the same time Sam boosted himself and Ivy up onto the surrounding ice sheet with one arm until only his booted feet remained submerged in the bay. Each yank on the rope drew them closer to the shore now, and thankfully the ice held beneath them. Once they were ashore, Riley dropped the rope and hobbled over to help him with Ivy.

"Adi," she told her niece. "Go back to the house and get my coat. We need something warm and dry to wrap Ivy in until the medics arrive."

The little girl raced back up the boardwalk.

Sirens echoed in the distance, but they were

still a few minutes out, if Riley had to guess.
Ivy's little face was blue from the cold as Riley
checked for a pulse. "She's unresponsive and not
breathing. Starting CPR now."

Riley gave two breaths, then Sam started chest
compressions on his daughter. Ivy's tiny chest
rose and fell with each ventilation, which only
made the stillness afterward that much more dis-
turbing.

"Come on, *yeobo*," Sam pleaded. "Breathe.
Please just take a breath."

They continued CPR until Ivy convulsed as
she choked. Riley turned the child over onto her
side where she coughed and vomited up seawater.
Adi had returned with her coat, and Riley took
it to wrap Ivy up in as the medics and fire rescue finally arrived. Sam was holding Ivy to him
now, rubbing her back as tears streamed down his
shivering face. "I thought I'd lost you too, *yeobo*."

Riley reached over to touch his arm as the
medics ran down to take over. "She's going to
be okay."

"I'm going with her to the ER," Sam said, stating
the obvious. He'd allowed Tate and the EMTs to
get Ivy onto a gurney and loaded into the back
of a nearby ambulance, but otherwise he was
in charge. He clutched the Mylar blanket they'd
given him tighter around himself and took a
large gulp of hot tea someone had shoved into

his hands after the chaos. Honestly, he could have been drinking sludge for all he tasted it. His attention was focused solely on his daughter now. No, that wasn't entirely true. He was also aware of Riley there, with her too-pale face and worried eyes. They'd been through hell just now and it showed. He didn't imagine he looked any better. But she'd stayed by his side through it all. Helping him save Ivy. He would never forget that. The EMTs gestured for him to get in the back of the ambulance with Ivy for the ride to the hospital, and he turned to Riley. They still had so much to say to each other, but now wasn't the time. "I'll call you once I know more."

She nodded and handed him back his phone. "I'll be praying for you and Ivy."

"Thanks." He wanted to say more, to apologize for everything that had happened since that party, to tell her how he felt, to ask her not to give up on him, on them, to beg her for another chance. But it would have to wait until later. So instead, he cupped her cheek, her skin cold beneath his touch. "Talk soon. Take care."

"You too," she said, turning her head slightly to kiss his palm. Then she stepped back beside Mark Bates, who was there with fire rescue.

His heart swelled with warmth as the doors closed and the rig took off, sirens blaring as they raced toward Wyckford General. The EMTs had replaced Riley's coat with heated blankets around

Ivy to keep her warm, and they'd started her on high-flow oxygen through a face mask, along with IV fluids—all routine care for drowning patients. They'd also done a preliminary exam for spinal injuries before loading her onto the gurney, but thankfully hadn't found any. She'd left Adi's waterlogged skates behind on the beach. He'd have to buy a new set for Adi, but it was a small price to pray for his daughter being alive and hopefully well.

Ivy wasn't talking, just gripping Sam's hand for dear life. His mind still raced with what-ifs. What if he'd not reached her in time? What if the CPR hadn't worked? What if she had permanent brain damage from being underwater so long, not breathing? Sam rubbed his eyes with his free hand, the Mylar blanket crinkling around him each time he moved.

"Okay, Doc?" Tate Griffin asked him.

"Yeah," Sam replied. While having an analytical mind was good on many levels, it could also turn against you at times, causing anxiety that fed on itself. It hadn't happened to Sam in a while, not since he'd left San Diego. But this near miss with Ivy had triggered him again. "Just exhausted."

As they neared the hospital, he wished Riley was there with him. Her ability to calm and refocus him was just another reason to love her. He froze at the realization. Yep. It was true.

I love Riley Turner.

Sam's eyes sprang open at the feel of Ivy squeezing his hand tighter. "What is it, *yeobo*? What do you need?" He brought her chilled hand to his lips to kiss it.

Ivy swallowed hard, the monitors she was hooked up to beeping as her core body temperature updated to ninety-five. A good sign. "I said, can Riley come live with us and be like another mommy for me?"

"Oh, uh…" Taken aback, Sam wasn't sure how to answer. He hadn't gotten that far yet, let alone heard Riley say she loved him too. Plus, marriage was a big deal. Did either of them even want that? He didn't know but wanted to reassure his daughter. "How about we talk about this later, after we get your prognosis."

Ivy wrinkled her nose. "What's a frogdosis?"

Sam laughed then, a mix of relief and thankfulness and tension release. "Prognosis. It means how well they expect you to recover."

"We're here, Doc," Tate said as they slowed to a halt.

The next several minutes passed in a blur as the back doors of the rig opened at the ER entrance to reveal Brock and nurse Madi Scott waiting for them. They got Ivy unloaded then Sam followed the team inside as Tate gave them a rundown of what had happened, Ivy's condition and the treatment so far. Sam only let go of Ivy's hand once when they moved her from the ambulance gurney to a hospital bed in one of the ER trauma rooms.

Sam stood to the side of the bed as Brock ran the team's assessment and treatment plan. There was a reason you didn't treat your own family members; it clouded your judgment, and he couldn't afford to make mistakes now.

"What's her O2 level?" Brock asked.

"Ninety-one percent," Madi said, checking the monitor as she helped remove Ivy's wet clothes before covering her with a gown and more blankets.

"Okay. Let's get an EKG to check for bradycardia, please." While Madi placed the pads on her small chest, Brock did a neurological check on Ivy. "Hey, kiddo. Can you tell me your name?"

"Ivy Perkins."

"Very good. And how old are you?"

"Seven."

"Excellent. What month is it?"

"December."

"And where do you live?"

"Wyckford, Massachusetts."

"Perfect."

Then Ivy added, "I used to live in San Diego, but then Mommy died, so Daddy and I moved here. It's nice. And Adi's my best friend!"

"Yes, she is." Brock grinned before winking at Sam, letting him know his daughter was okay. "GCS score of fifteen."

"Is Riley your sister?" Ivy asked Brock, frowning.

"Yes."

"You were yelling at her at the party."

Brock stopped and looked from Ivy to Sam then back again. "I was. And that was wrong of me. I shouldn't have done that."

"No, you shouldn't," Ivy scolded him. "I get in trouble when I yell at people."

Brock glanced up at Sam again, this time biting his lips as if holding back a smile. To Ivy he said, "Yelling is hardly ever a good thing to do. Especially with my sister."

Ivy seemed to think about that for a moment before asking, "Are you still mad at her?"

"No. Not anymore. I wasn't mad at her anyway." He shrugged. "But I need to apologize to her."

"I like Riley. I asked Daddy if she can be my new mommy," Ivy told him before Sam could stop her.

All eyes suddenly turned to him again, but instead of feeling exposed, this time Sam puffed out his chest and stood tall. He loved Riley and he didn't care if the world knew. He and Brock had a mini standoff across the bed, then Brock finally lifted his chin slightly in a show of acceptance and a bit of the tension still lingering inside Sam relaxed.

Brock continued with the exam, asking Ivy to breathe as he used his stethoscope on her chest and back. "Some rales noted on left side on exam. Slight cough observed. Signs of aspiration. How's the EKG looking, Madi?"

"So far, so good," Madi said, checking the strip. "No dysrhythmias noted."

"Great." Brock examined Ivy's abdomen next. "And no gastric distention. Let's get a core body temp on her and an initial chest X-ray to check for delayed or developing pulmonary edema. Pending those results, we'll repeat it again after eight hours to check for any changes. Also, get a blood glucose and ABG from the lab. Classify her as a grade two drowning and let's put her on observation and monitor her condition until the next chest X-ray. Keep her hydrated and warm under observation until then, please. Thanks, everyone."

Brock then took Sam to a small conference room across the hall and closed the door. "I owe you an apology."

"I don't care about that right now. I just want to know my daughter will be okay," he said, sitting on a chair against the wall. His clothes were still damp, and his boots squished with each step. He hadn't taken time to change after the rescue. All his focus had been on saving Ivy.

"We'll know more after the observation period. Symptom development can be delayed because of the hypothermia," Brock said, walking over to a nearby cabinet and pulling out a fresh set of scrubs and a pair of hospital socks, the kind they usually gave patients to wear. He handed it all to Sam. "Get warm and dry, then we'll talk more, okay? I'm due for a break, so I'll buy you a coffee in the cafeteria."

He left without waiting for Sam's answer, meaning it wasn't up for discussion. So be it. The guy would be Sam's new brother-in-law if things went to plan, so he needed this to go well. He took off his sodden clothes and boots and exchanged them for the fresh scrubs and socks, then found an empty plastic bag to store his wet stuff in until he could get it home. Once he was done, he went back out to check on Ivy before joining Brock at the nurses' station to head downstairs. He could use the caffeine to keep awake, since it sounded like they'd be there a while.

"So, you and my sister aren't just a fling? You're a couple now?" Brock waited until they got their drinks and found a table in a quiet part of the cafeteria to bring up the subject, not far from where he'd sat with Riley that one late night that felt like forever ago. "How long has that been going on?"

"Not long." Sam shrugged, wincing slightly at the pain in his shoulder. He was going to feel the rescue in the morning. "And we're not a couple. I mean, I'd like to be, but I'm not sure that's what she wants now, so…"

"You talked to her at her house earlier?" Brock's expression remained frustratingly neutral, so Sam couldn't read whether he was happy about the news. Based on the fight at the party the other day, it was hard to tell.

"I did, but the way we left things…" He scrubbed a hand over his face. "I don't know where things stand with us."

"Riley is my only sibling, Sam. And despite going at it sometimes, we take care of each other." He toyed with his cup of coffee, scowling down at the dark liquid inside. "She's been through a lot. I just want to make sure she's protected."

"I know. Me too," Sam said. "I've been through some things too."

"Well, despite what's happened in your pasts, I saw how Riley looked at you, like you're her favorite present, and I saw the same goofy expression on your face too, so maybe give it another try. Love isn't necessarily easy, but it's always worth it, if it's real."

Sam was too tired for this. "I know. I know it's worth it. But I'm still trying to wrap my analytical brain around the fact that for some crazy reason, I seem to have fallen hard for your sister after only a couple of weeks. But we just feel right together. And no matter how hard I try to logic my way out of it, that's the truth. Have you ever felt that way about anyone? Like fate had brought you together?"

Brock snorted. "Cassie and I were only back together a few weeks too when I knew."

Sam sat back and sighed. "I care for Riley, and I want a future with her, however that looks for us. I never expected to find love again after my wife died, but my past has taught me how precious it is. I don't want to lose this chance with her."

Brock smiled at last. "You're a good man, Sam. And while I don't appreciate you two sneaking around behind my back at my house, I think you two will be good for each other. And Ivy is a pure joy. It's not easy being a dad on your own, is it?" He sat back as well, shaking his head. "I'm not gonna lie. It nearly killed me. I felt like I was stretched too thin to be any good to anyone who mattered. Hell, it got to the point my daughter wasn't even talking like a human anymore."

Sam snorted. "Riley told me."

"Then Cassie came back to town, and she somehow broke through all that noise. Don't ask me how, but she did. I've always believed when you know, you know."

Sam took that in then sat forward to check his watch. "You really think Ivy will be fine?"

"I do." Brock switched back into doctor mode again. "She's very lucky. The cold water helped her. Slowed everything down until help arrived. You're a hero, Dr. Perkins."

"Can I get that in writing, please?" Sam laughed. "Might come in handy when I start the renovations on your sister's new house."

Brock chuckled. "She'll still be salty some-times."

"I wouldn't have her any other way."

They finished their drinks then returned up-stairs. Brock went to grab a new patient while Sam returned to Ivy's room to sit by her bedside while she slept. She looked as tired as Sam felt, but at least she was alive and well. He pulled out his phone from his pocket to check his emails and found a text from Riley.

Just checking on you. Hope everything's okay.

That heart emoji at the end made him smile.

He sent her back a quick text telling her they were okay, with a smiley face at the end, then settled into his chair for a nap.

He didn't get to sleep long, however, before he heard Ivy's small voice say, "I'm sorry, Daddy. I just wanted to see what it was like out there. It was cold. It was so cold. And dark." Tears trick-led down her cheeks. "I tried to yell when I fell in, but it was like the ice squeezed all the sound out of me."

"Don't cry, *yeobo*," he said, leaning in to kiss the top of her head. "It's all going to be okay."

Ivy was quite for a while, so long that Sam wondered if she'd fallen asleep again. But then she looked at him, her expression serious. "Adi says that you like her aunt Riley."

Sam had wondered how he'd talk about with his daughter, but it seemed fate had intervened yet again. "I do. Very much. In fact, I love her."

"You do?" Ivy looked up at him again. "So we'll be a family again?"

"I hope so." His chest squeezed with sweetness.

They sat there for a while as Ivy seemed to process that. Then she asked, "Can I still be in the Christmas play tomorrow?"

He'd forgotten all about that with everything going on. It was twenty-four hours away, and he'd have to double-check with Brock to be sure, but if he cleared Ivy, Sam would be okay with it. He told his daughter as much.

"Yay!" She clapped. "I'm going to be the best goldfish ever!"

They settled back into quiet again after that, Ivy snoozing while Sam sorted through things in his head. It was still hard for his analytical side to grasp how quickly things had happened in his life here. Riley had brought light and warmth to his life, just like she had to all the people she cared for. She had made him smile, laugh, *feel* again.

He remembered something Cassie Turner had told him once when she'd first persuaded him to move to Wyckford almost two years prior. She'd given up everything to return home and marry Brock, basically starting all over again, just like Sam.

I realized my life would never be what I'd once planned, but that didn't mean it was over.

Sam knew now that was true for him as well. He still had things to do and people to love—one very determined, very independent, very passionate radiologist.

And sure, she was salty sometimes, but he could be a difficult person to live with too, fussy and exacting to a fault. But the past few years had taught him it wasn't so much the differences that mattered; it was the ways you were alike with someone. Control was a fallacy, one he'd chased for far too long. Much better to take what came your way and make it better, support those around you and stand strong through good times and bad. That's what survivors did.

He closed his eyes again, wholly overwhelmed at the idea of a future with Riley. She'd given her all today to help rescue Ivy and it meant the world to him. His spirts lifted, buoyant like a helium balloon. He and Riley had things to talk about. Not over text, but face-to-face. Baring his soul was not in his nature, but for a chance at forever with Riley, he knew he had to open his heart to her completely and risk it all for love.

The next night, Riley dressed in her favorite red sweater and jeans for the Christmas play, then looked at herself in the mirror. She hadn't seen Sam or Ivy since the accident, and while they'd texted updates to each other since then, she was anxious to see them with her own eyes to make sure they were all right. Sam had seemed oddly vague with details, so she wasn't sure what to expect.

"Riley?" Brock called from the living room. "Get a move on!"

"I'm coming," she yelled back. "Be there in a minute."

Speaking of squirrelly, her brother had been acting weird too. They'd made up after their fight, they always did, but he was also vague whenever she asked him questions about Sam and Ivy, giving her only the driest of details. Which only made her nerves worse.

Things between her and Sam hadn't exactly been going swimmingly before Ivy fell through the ice. In fact, she'd called it off completely at the party, so she couldn't really blame him for being chilly toward her now. She'd hurt him badly, when she'd known he really had only been trying to help. He wasn't a do-gooder. He'd shown her in so many small ways over the past few weeks that she was more than her injuries. Shown her that true freedom sometimes meant forging connections with others. And now she realized just how much she loved Sam. But she'd ended it all herself—over before it had really started because of her stupid hang-ups about independence.

Sam didn't want to steal her freedom; he wanted to support her so she could soar.

With a sad sigh, Riley grabbed her coat and bag and joined the others in the living room, all too aware of Brock watching her, eagle-eyed. She'd deal with it, whatever happened, because that's what she did. But there would always be a Sam-sized hole in her heart.

As Brock helped her with her coat, he gave her a sidelong look. "Everything okay?"

"Fine," she said flatly. "We're going to see goldfish in Bethlehem."

Brock looked concerned, but thankfully didn't push it.

At the school, Riley forced a cheerful smile until she thought her face might crack. Adi's teacher had saved them seats in the crowded school gymnasium, near the aisle for Riley's wheelchair. Brock rushed Adi backstage while Riley sat out front with Cassie. The place was packed, standing room only, as she scanned the crowd for Sam. She spotted him a few rows ahead, sitting with Hala and her husband. Riley tried to get his attention, but he kept his attention on the program in his hands.

Brock found them just as the light went down and the play started. While the play progressed, Riley did her best to focus on the stage instead of Sam in front of her. The Nativity production

ended up being adorable, complete will a pleth-
ora of animals and sea creatures from all over the
globe that couldn't have possibly ever been in the
ancient Middle East, but they increased the number of parts so every child in school had a role
onstage. There was even had a sing-along, with
all the standard carols and the audience encour-
aged to participate.

After the pageant was over, everyone returned
to the lobby to enjoy light refreshments, but Riley
stayed behind, making some lame excuse about
needing to call the hospital for something. Sam
stayed too, she noticed, and she couldn't stand
the suspense anymore, so she unlocked her chair
wheels and rolled down to see him. She stopped
about a foot away from him and met his gaze, her
pulse tripping anew as she saw all the emotions
there. So many things she hadn't dared hope for
but wanted so badly from him—care, devotion,
respect, love. That last one stole her breath.

"Hey," Sam said, his voice a tad husky. "How'd
you like the play?"

"It was great. How's Ivy?"

"Good."

"And how do you feel?"

"Sore," he said, rolling a shoulder then wincing. "I'm getting too old for that stuff."

She bit her lip. "Do you really want to talk
about the play?"

"No," he said, reaching over to pull her onto his lap before she even realized what he was doing. At first Riley froze, then she relaxed into him, his arms around her waist as she pulled back to see his face, concerned. "You're shaking."

He tucked her head beneath his chin, rocking her back and forth gently, as if she were the most precious thing in the world to him. Her heart grew three sizes bigger with love for him too as she buried her face into the base of his neck. "Better now," he whispered against the top of her head. "I missed you."

"I missed you too," she said, eyes closed. "I'm so sorry for what I said to you at the party. I never meant to hurt you. I was angry and frustrated with the situation and I lashed out, but it wasn't your fault. I'll do better in the future."

"It's okay. I should have given you space in that moment. I knew that's what you needed, but my need to help overrode my common sense." Eventually, he leaned back and cupped her cheeks, bringing her gaze to his. "So I'm sorry too. And we'll both do better. Together. Thank you for helping to save my daughter. Thank you for seeing me and bringing light back into my life. I love you, Riley Turner, and I want a future with you. Ivy does too. She's crazy about you too. Will you have us?"

She blinked to clear the tears gathering in her

eyes, the cracks in her heart that had been there for years now beginning to mend. "Say it again."

"I love you."

She kissed him then, only to pull away when a chorus of cheers and applause echoed from the lobby. Riley looked over Sam's shoulder to see their friends and family and half the town in the doorway, watching them. Riley laughed, burying her face in his shoulder. "Well, I guess the secret's out now."

"Guess so." Sam pulled her closer and kissed her again, seemingly not caring at all.

This time when she pulled away, Riley was breathless with wonder and hope. "I love you too, Sam. I thought doing everything by myself made me strong, but now I realize that without connection, without people I care for supporting me, I can't do anything. I can't wait to create forever with you and Ivy. And I can't believe I saw you for over a year and never took much notice, then boom. Feelings!" Pressed up against him as she was, her heart pounding in time with his, Riley never wanted to move again. "And I adore Ivy too. Of course I'll have you both."

Sam's embrace tightened around her as he kissed her again. "Good. Now tell me what you want for Christmas."

She shook her head, smiling from ear to ear. "Nothing. I have everything I want."

"Me too." Sam smiled then kissed her once

more, and Riley put *everything* into it—her promise to be with him always, her hope for the future, her forever love for him and Ivy. Her very own family of three under the tree.

EPILOGUE

One year later...

"ARE YOU SURE we'll have enough popcorn?" Riley asked, her tone sarcastic.

Sam made a face at her from across the massive island in their new kitchen, which was currently covered in enough red-and-white-striped popcorn bags to feed an army.

"I only made ten batches," he said defensively. He'd spent a lot of time calculating just how much they'd need. "We have twenty guests coming, so that should be about right. Everyone loves popcorn, so I think we'll be lucky to have a kernel left over for ourselves."

"Better grab one now then, I guess." She shrugged, adjusting her crutches to grab the nearest bag.

"Help yourself," Sam said, distracted. Now that he was looking at it, maybe his calculations had been wrong. "Actually, maybe I better make another batch..."

He'd just added more popcorn kernels to the popper when he felt Riley's arms around his waist. "On second thought, it's not popcorn I'm craving," she murmured, kissing the back of his neck until he shivered.

They'd been engaged six months now and were still going strong. Sam couldn't get enough of her, and the feeling seemed to be mutual. He turned to kiss her, careful to avoid banging into one of her crutches. She was using them more than the chair now. To say Sam was impressed was the understatement of the century. He knew how hard she'd worked to get here, and he was so proud of her he could burst.

Riley pulled away slightly. "When is everyone coming again?"

"Fifteen minutes. Not enough time for what you're thinking."

"Damn." She slid away again to look out the window over the sink.

He and Ivy had settled even more into life in Wyckford since moving in with Riley. Now, in addition to his duties as head of neurosurgery at Wyckford General and his ALS research project, he also spearheaded a local charity called Natalia's Place, dedicated to providing accessibility resources and home renovations for those in need in the area. Everyone should be comfortable and safe where they lived, and it gave Sam a chance to donate his handyman skills to a good cause.

A win-win for everyone.

Riley was still busy as ever at the hospital and with helping to raise Ivy. The two had bonded even more, with Ivy calling Riley her "S-Mom," short for "second mom." It made Sam's heart so happy to know his daughter, *their* daughter, had someone as kind and loyal and strong as Riley in her corner.

He leaned his hips back against the kitchen counter while the corn popped and caught Riley as she passed by him, pulling her close once more. Having everyone over to their newly renovated place for the first time was a big deal, and he felt a little nervous.

"Stop worrying," she ordered him. "You already know everyone loves you. And they're going to love the house too. It's gorgeous. You did an amazing job!"

He took a deep breath and realized it was true. He and Ivy were a part of this town now, and it was a part of them. They made a difference in the lives of the people around them, and that was all Sam had ever wanted. Well, that and Riley, whom Sam loved with all his heart and soul. She felt the same about him. He knew because she told him every day. Told Ivy too. They'd truly become a family.

"Thank you," he said, resting his forehead against Riley's.

"For?" she asked, her dark brows furrowing.

"A million things. Mostly for not giving up on me when all this started."

Sam kissed her fast, letting her go just as Ivy came into the kitchen.

"I can't wait to see Adi," Ivy said, clapping. "When will she be here?"

Riley looked at the clock in the kitchen. "Soon. Looks like it's snowing again, so they may have slowed down because of the weather."

"Yeah. Daisy texted and said she and her mother might be a little late for that reason."

"Better safe than sorry," Riley said.

"That's what I told her."

Daisy was holding her own right now, not getting any better, but not getting any worse either. She worked from home now as a web designer rather than going into an office and overall was making the best of her circumstances. She'd also joined a support group at the hospital, to talk about her experiences and share resources with others in similar situations.

"How's the book coming?" Sam asked his daughter.

Ivy sighed. The therapist she'd started seeing after her fall through the ice had suggested journaling for Ivy, to work out her trauma over the accident and her grief over losing her mother. "Writing is hard."

"No lies detected there," Riley said.

"Do I have to do it?"

Sam shrugged. "You don't have to, but maybe if you take some time away then come back to it, you might feel differently."

"Maybe." Ivy seemed like eight going on eighteen sometimes, and Sam shuddered at the thought of impending teenager-hood in a few short years. The doorbell rang then, and Ivy jumped. "I'll get it!"

A moment later, his daughter led the new arrivals into the kitchen—Brock and Adi, followed by Cassie with their baby. Brock carried a large plate covered in plastic wrap balanced on one hand.

"Sorry we're late." Cassie looked around the kitchen. "The roads were a bit dicey. This place looks beautiful!"

"Thank you," Sam said, taking the plate from Brock and unwrapping it to find brownies before setting it on the island where people could help themselves to snacks. "And I'm glad you made it safely. Please make yourselves comfortable. We figured we'd wait until everyone was here to give the grand tour."

Brock kissed Riley on the cheek before grabbing a beer from the fridge. "Great work, Sam."

For the next half hour, a steady stream of people crowded into the house. Madi and Tate. Luna and Mark. Cassie's dad, Ben. Daisy and her mother. Even Lucille and grumpy old Mr. Martin. Once everyone had arrived, taken the tour, then settled into the living room with their popcorn and snacks, Sam moved to the front of the room near the large flat-screen TV and cleared his throat.

He looked out at everyone and thought about how empty his life would have been if he'd not taken that final, huge risk and opened his heart and soul to Riley, to the people of this town. Sam felt immeasurably blessed. "Thank you all for coming. These past couple of years have been a lot for me and Ivy and Riley, and we just want to thank you all for being there for us. We hope we can return the favor, and tonight is just a gift from us to you. Enjoy the show!"

Then he took his seat beside Riley on the sofa, Ivy on his other side, and Riley squeezed his hand at the cheerful opening credits rolled on *It's a Wonderful Life*. No matter what the future held for any of them, they had everything they needed right here in this room, all of it built on a foundation of love.

* * * * *

If you missed the previous story in the
Wyckford General Hospital quartet,
then check out

Her Forbidden Firefighter

And if you enjoyed this story,
check out these other great reads from
Traci Douglass

An ER Nurse to Redeem Him
Home Alone with the Children's Doctor
Single Dad's Unexpected Reunion

All available now!